OCTAVIA

OCTAVIA

MELINDA SELMYS

vulgata

To the best of my knowledge, all copyrighted works referenced in this book have been quoted in accord with accepted standards of fair use. If you are a copyright holder and I have used your work in a way that you don't like, or I have presumed excessively on your generosity, please notify me so that the problem may be rectified in future printings.

All characters appearing in this work are fictitious. Any resemblance to real persons, living, dead, or undead is purely coincidental, but kinda cool.

Octavia was written with Melinda's husband Chris, but his name didn't look good on the cover.

Octavia is Book I of the Kirkman Decalogue.

ISBN 978-0-9919098-5-8

For Agnes.

Once upon a time there was a girl named Octavia and a boy named William. They were looking for Roman ruins in the woods but they never found any because they were nowhere near ancient Rome. What they did find was a sunken well. For over a year it was their secret place and they played there every day. They never showed it to anyone else. William told all of his secrets to Octavia near that well, and when they were told he would take a stone and they would each put it in their mouths. William said that now the secret was held in the stone. He would throw the stone down the well.

One day, when the well was full of secrets, Willam fell in.

OCTAVIA

PROLOGUE

I am named Octavia because I am the youngest of eight children. My parents waited, patiently, until they had given birth to eight in order to bestow this name. I once asked whether they would have been disappointed if I were a boy, but they pointed out that Octavian is a no less illustrious and well-omened name than my own.

It was early morning and I was out in my front yard, washing my feet in the dew. This was a practice that I had adopted sometime in childhood, and I had secretly never given it up. Mist lay heavy on the pastures surrounding the old farmhouse and clung to the patches of blue-green grass that grew thickly underfoot. It gave sustenance to the beetles and the spiders.

I was watching the first rays of sunlight playing on the webs above the porch swing when I heard the sound of gravel crunching on the drive. Guiltily startled, I slipped on my dew-drenched shoes. I was sixteen now: too old to be caught indulging in such childish pleasures. Quickly, I began to gather flowers for the morning offering.

My brother, Germanicus, was walking up the path that leads from the barn. His t-shirt was drenched in blood, torn open at the front, and he had something horned and bloody draped across his shoulders. I blinked my eyes several times to banish the gory vision, but had to accept that it was reality. I ran to get a better look.

The thing around his shoulders was a young goat which had been white in its previous life. He had settled it there in such a way that it almost looked as if it might be sleeping, its head nestled up against his right ear, except that every so often his step jiggled in such a way that the long, deep slit in its throat gaped a little and fresh blood seeped out of the wound.

"Did you kill that yourself?"

"Yes."

"Why didn't you drive it down to the abbatoire?"

"Hiring a hit man is the same as doing the deed yourself: it's just less honorable."

"But I thought that you were a vegetarian."

"Yeah. But that's a matter of discipline, not principle. Besides, I was starting to worry that it might just be a matter of sentimentality." He patted the bloodied flanks of the goat. "I've now confirmed that I am definitely not squeamish. You want to help me butcher it?"

I looked at the poor thing. There was something uncannily peaceful and reconciled about its expression, which disturbed me. "No thanks," I said, "I think I am squeamish."

"That's too bad. I thought we might open up its gut and read the auspices. A little amateur augury to get the day started."

It was typical of my brother's sense of humor that I couldn't tell whether he was joking or not, and there was always the possibility that he was joking, but that his joke would include actually fishing around in the intestines of the poor thing. "You can tell me later whether the omens were good or bad."

IV

He loaded the carcasse into the back of the pick-up and drove down the winding lane that leads to our slaughterhouse. It was an old truck, so heavily rusted that the Ontario government would no longer license it for use on the road. I finished gathering my bouquets: fiery *lobelias*, nodding fall asters and pale crook-necked lustrife. I skipped up the steps that led back into the house.

The *lares*, our tutelary gods, lived just inside the front door in a room that had once-upon-a-time been a porch but now doubled as a coat-room and a shrine. I placed the flowers on the altars, mumbled a quick prayer for their protection, and then changed into my Wellies before heading out to feed the geese.

Down by the pond, the sumac trees were leaning their green, feathered leaves towards the banks. Rosy-fingered dawn was slipping back into sleepy obscurity, and Apollo had started to draw the sun up into the sky. Several tame geese looked at me lazily, their heads still half-tucked beneath their ivory wings. I scattered crumbs along the edge of the water, then sat to watch them eat.

Germanicus joined me just as they were finishing their breakfast. He had washed his hands, but his clothing still looked like a costume from a bad horror movie. "You want some coffee?" he said, proffering a mug. "I mixed it gross and milky-sweet, just how you like it."

He took his coffee midnight-black, but he'd mixed mine up okay. "So," I poked him, "how are the auspices today?"

V

A long, thready, drawn-out breath. "Actually, the auspices are weird. I mean, not that I actually believe in that kind of thing, but..."

"But?" I leaned forward. I did believe in that kind of thing.

"I chose that goat because it seemed to be in some kind of in distress. I figured I'd put it out of it's misery. But when I opened it up I found this creepy stone inside." It was small, black, volcanic, with a sharp point and something etched into the side. "I can't imagine why it would have swallowed that. Not unless someone forced it to."

I snatched it to get a better look. The marking was what I hoped: clumsily carved, but recognizable. A W inside of an O. Tears welled up before I could suppress them and I had to pretend that I was being sentimental about the goat. "Poor thing. It must have been in pain."

"Yeah, well it's dead now." Germanicus had adopted his *memento mori* asana, and I was afraid that he was never going to leave. Or worse, that he would try to get the stone back before he went. I knew there was only one person that stone could have come from. But William had been gone six years now, lost at the bottom of a well. No way could he have survived. And yet...

After an eternity that lasted a few seconds, my brother wandered off. As soon as he was out of sight, I placed the stone on my tongue. It brought back a very old memory.

VI

ACT I

WOULD YOU SCREAM

We had been ten years old. The woods were different then: the footprints that ran this way and that across the paths of our childhood had belonged to goblins and Sasquatch. There had been secret passageways through the trees and ancient fortresses built on tumbling hills. It had been possible, at any moment, to take the wrong step, the ill-fated turning off out of the real and into the dim, wonderful and terrifying realms of Faerie.

William had known this better than me on some deep, intuitive level, but he had not understood what he had known. He would come to a place on the path and would stop suddenly, looking back and forth, up and down, his small, black-haired serious head peering into the spaces between worlds, alert, pale, frightened. I was the one who told him about how it was; that Odysseus had found the secret place where it was possible to go and talk to the spirits of the dead, how Orpheus had gone down into Hades to rescue his beloved Eurydice, how Jove might, at any moment, come swooping down on the wings of an eagle or a swan to bear you aloft to the halls of high Olympus. Fairy tales had never filled his childhood, a place where entertainments came in the form of a brightly flickering television set and the distant voices of his parents in the room beyond. A house of separate rooms, where stories were all about frogs and turtles making friends and sharing toys. He had devoured the rich mythological heritage of Greece and Rome from my mind with a ferocity that had frightened me.

"Tell me another one," he said.

I scoured my brain. "I don't know this one very well," I apologized. My diction was precise in a way that impressed adults and kept most other children at bay. William was one of the few exceptions. "It's about a girl who was the daughter of a goddess. She was very beautiful. The leaves and the flowers used to come up out of the ground where she walked."

"Are all beautiful women in the other world like that?" William asked. I was surprised by the turn of phrase, 'the other world.' I had never thought of it that way. To me a centaur might be something that was really lurking around the next corner, skittishly running away. It wasn't a part of a separate reality.

"It's a common motif," I said, proud of the word 'motif' which had just been taught to me by my big brother Augustus.

"Go on, go on."

"Well, one day she was out walking in the wide world, and all of the birds were following her and singing, and flowers were growing, and everything was very nice. But then there was a big earthquake, and the ground opened up like a hungry mouth, and it spit out a chariot. A black chariot, driven by black horses, and sitting in the front of it, holding a whip and a frothing glass of black wine, was the God of the Underworld, Pluto." This was embellished, but I was a good embellisher. My teachers all said so.

"Was he like the devil?" William demanded.

"Oh no, nothing like the devil. The devil is ugly and red and has horns on his head. Pluto was very beautiful, only a terrible kind of beautiful. The way that sometimes a wolf is beautiful, or a scary path on a dark night. He scooped up the girl, whose name was Persephone. She screamed and screamed so loudly that everything in the whole world could hear her. But there was nothing, not a single person, not a boy, not a girl, or a man, or a woman, or even a bear or an eagle, who was brave enough to come to her rescue. She was swept away like a sandcastle in the tide and taken down into the dark, dark depths of the earth. He made her be a queen there. The queen of the underworld."

"Had she done something wrong? Something to deserve it?"

"Only being beautiful."

"That's not wrong, I don't think. Sometimes beautiful people think they're better than everyone else. Was Persephone like that?"

He was talking about Cataline, his older sister. "No," I said, "Persephone was nothing like that. She was beautiful and good and she had done nothing to deserve it. That's why when she was taken down into the darkness the entire world began to weep. The trees refused to bear fruit. The grass lay down in the sun and died. The fields were all eaten up by fire. Even the animals wouldn't get up and eat or have babies or anything. The sun became cold, and snow fell for the first time, and everything was covered up with sorrow. That was the first winter ever."

"Do you think," William asked, "that if I went down into the darkness, that there would be a tree that would refuse to bear fruit?"

"Probably`," I said. "I think that there is such a tree for every person who lives." I was making it up, but it sounded romantic.

He looked thoughtful. "If Pluto came up out of the earth, right here, right now, and promised to make you a princess in another world, would you go with him, or would you scream and scream until the whole earth heard you?"

"I would scream, of course. Otherwise, I would never see my mother and father again. Or any of my brothers and sisters. Wouldn't you?"

William shrugged and looked off, down a path in the woods that wasn't there. "It's hard to say," he said. "You never know."

ALL WILL BE WELL

The stone lay on my bedside table, its glassy surface catching the wan light of my candle. Outside a fat, lazy moon slung herself back in a hammock of stars. The candle was scented with purifying herbs that were supposed to keep dark spirits away. So far, it wasn't helping. Every time I lay down to sleep I could feel a dream trying to have me – an old, old dream that I hadn't had in a long time.

I sat up in bed and tried to write some poetry. The muses, however, had long since gone to sleep and all of my attempts were drippy and insipid. Finally I gathered my failed verses in a ball and went downstairs in search of a fellow insomniac.

XVI

The soft light of the refrigerator played with the shadows of the fire burning in the stove; it was not cold, but my mother was fermenting something with a rich, fishy, Mediterranean smell. Just as we were all required to pretend we lived in ancient Rome, the kitchen had to make believe that it was a sun-swept dock in the port of Ostia.

I could see my father's light on in his study down the hall.

I added the poems to the fire, armed myself with a glass of milk, and then went and knocked softly on the study door, hoping that it wouldn't wake him if he had fallen asleep with the light on. The door opened. I don't know how: my father was sitting still at his desk on the opposite side of the room and didn't look as though he had moved at all. He has always opened his door to us in this way, ever since I was a child, and none of us have ever figured out how it is done.

"I couldn't sleep," I said, settling myself on the old chesterfield with its rough, brown-and yellow upholstery, its musty smell, and its hidden reserves of ancient and forever-lost treasures. I wanted to tell him about my nightmares but the words stuck in my throat.

My father smiled. "Come and sit down. I will read to you from the Aeneid, as a proper father should." He pulled a volume down from the shelf. Its spine cracked, spilling out several loose pages onto the floor, he gathered them up and lovingly replaced them, musing to himself, "You know, I've always thought it a shame that I couldn't have you children suckled by wolves."

I smiled a sleepy smile and took a sip of milk and didn't mention that anything was wrong.

He opened Virgil, and began to read, the long, lilting Latin syllables running together, totally incomprehensible to me at 4 in the morning. I pulled the blanket down off the back of the couch and curled up, soothing myself by braiding and unbraiding my hair. As the magic of milk and poetry slowly lulled me back to sleep, the dream began.

It was always the same. First, the darkness. Then a smell like algae and rotten leaves. Finally, lights twinkling in the distance, faltering, secretive, like selfish stars trying to keep their sparkle to themselves. I sat and the sitting seemed to take forever. I could feel the world revolving beneath me, but it was a small world, a rusted ball-bearing in a vast machine. A grinding sound arose with each revolution, and then turned into a buzzing like the sound of angry bees.

No, not bees. Moths. They swept around me like a draft down a chimney, innumerable silver wings beating the air. Their fragile bodies were covered in sheer, chitinous plating and if you looked you could see that inside they were empty, filled with stagnant air. I covered my nose, my mouth, my eyes, to keep them out. They crawled across my skin, and then were gone.

This is when I changed. I was no longer myself, but William: still ten years old, with a spectral, reedy voice. My eyes were clockwork and I had copper veins that carried light through my body like blood. I sang nursery rhymes to myself, and they echoed from stone that was close as skin.

I woke with a start. The sunlight was flooding in through my father's window. I sat up to find a book of poetry sitting on the bedside table, leaning against a cup of fresh goat's milk. It was an old book, cloth-bound, with yellowed pages and flowers pressed between the leaves. *Beloved Poems*, was what the title page read. There was an inscription inside, "For my daughter, Octavia, who has bad dreams." Then a page number. I flipped to the page, which was in the middle of a poem called Little Gidding. My father, in neat black pen-strokes had underlined a verse:

And all shall be well and
All manner of things shall be well

MAGICIAN'S CHOICE

A large bell, deep-bellied, peels out across a plain in darkness. Once upon a time, William thought of the dark as complete, unbroken, but his eyes have grown accustomed to it and now he can see that there is a sort of settlement down there, on the other side of the river, below the bell-tower. It's lights are many coloured, but they drown in the blackness -- the way a Christmas tree might look like if it were sunk down in a swamp.

The evening bells are William's job, and it's very important. Here, where there is no day or night, the way that you make time is with the bell. It creates a morning and a noon, a time for dinner and a time for sleep. Right now, William has just made it into bedtime.

Slowly, dragging the toes of his shoes along the ground as he walks, he heads towards the bridge. From here you can hear the rushing of the river. William remembers the first time he saw this bridge, garlanded in bright crystals that gave off a bluish light. Then, the lights sparkled on the waters and you could see that there were shadow-fish down there, swimming. But now the bridge-lights were dim, like the last faint echo of light in an old glow-in-the-dark sticker, and William knew that they would not brighten again until someone new came to live in the Well.

On the far side of the bridge, the path winds down into the arboretum where stones hang ripening on the crooked limbs of copper trees. They aren't real trees, of course. Plants cannot live down here, being deprived of the sunlight. But the children who inhabit the well have made their own gardens of hammered brass and twisted copper-wire. They are beautiful in their way, but dead. Even the clouds of perfume that hang here, suspended on the stagnant air, always smell like they've come from a bottle.

William plucks a stone from one of the trees and carries it into the millyard. Here a huge revolving globe of basalt sits in a granite basin, ready to grind tomorrow's stone. A chute brings the stone down to the sluices, where they are bathed in tears to reveal their worth. Little Yvette is carefully putting screens over the sluices to make sure that nothing comes during sleeptime to drink up the tears.

XXI

William rushes past her, past the storehouses, into the garden. Here the trees are laden with multi-coloured fruits -- each of them a work of art made by one of the older girls: hand-carved apples, plums and pomegranates meticulously covered in a mosaic of glowing stone. They're getting a little dim now, but in the morning someone will mist them with sorrow and they will glow anew.

Antonio is here, dressed in a shabby old suit and an opera cape that's hundreds of years old. Behind him is a stone portico that leads down into the earth. They sleep underground, in the caverns, because it's safer there. A curtain of blue-stone, sharp crystals that cling to razor-fine copper wires, hangs down to block the entrance. There is also a large copper grate that Antonio will close up once everyone is inside.

William sits down on the swing and gives himself a little push with his legs to get it going. Overhead, the coloured fruits reel in and out of sight like lanterns at a carnival.

"It's time for bed," Antonio reminds him.

Yvette comes rushing through, "*Desolée*," she says, courtsying slightly as she skips past. With an almost scurrying motion, she flees down the hole.

Antonio begins to move the copper grate, very slowly, looking at William, "Do you wish to stay outside?"

"I haven't decided yet." William likes it out here: the loneliness, the quiet, the danger. There are so many

XXII

unanswered questions, experiments to be run. He's tired though. Maybe safety would be best.

There's a sound of slapping bare feet coming along the stone path. Jules emerges from the darkness. He looks to be a very tiny eight-year-old, but he lived in the 1700s. He's chewing on a piece of sausage and William can smell that it isn't Well-food. His mouth waters as much with jealousy as with hunger. Alone among all of the children, Jules is able to return back to the upworld. Antonio says it's because when he disappeared there was noone left behind to remember or to grieve him, but William can see that this answer is incomplete.

Jules slows down, stuffs the last bite of meat into his mouth and slouches past. Antonio stops him and asks him something in French.

"Oui, Papa," Jules sounds bored. "C'est finis." He shuffles off towards the dormitories where already the other children are settling off to sleep.

Antonio looks at William. "Perhaps we should stay out a moment longer." He crosses over to a low, copper bush that nestles against the wall of the dining hall. There are roses there, made of all different alloys so that each one has a particular shade of its own. Little coils of paper are tied to the branches, messages of encouragement for whomever might be sad. Antonio settles himself on a low metal bench amid the flowers.

William stops the swing and listens, trying to be patient. At last, no longer able to contain himself, he bursts

XXIII

out, "What is it, Papa?" He almost never calls Antonio by that name, even though all of the other children do. But something in this moment endears him to the man.

Antonio's smile is deep-creased, sinking into the shadows where sorrow has mined his face. "The time is propitious," he says. "Your message has been delivered. Jules has seen it in Octavia's hands."

William's heart, for the first time in six years, swells with something akin to hope. "And then she'll come?" he cries. "Now that she's found it?"

Antonio smiles, sure that he has picked his moment perfectly. "Oh, she might," he says. "She will have what we call...a magician's choice."

BELOVED SON

There is disagreement between my parents as to whether or not we children are allowed to read the Christian Bible. My mother is against it on the basis that Christianity is an effeminate slave religion that brought down the Empire, and also because Lydia, who married a Catholic, has already been seduced to the dark side. My father is in favor on the basis that Jesus of Nazareth has a compelling philosophy, and you can't understand the last 2000 years of Western culture and history without it. The compromise position is that we are allowed to read St. Jerome's Vulgate in order to practice our Latin.

XXV

This means that Germanicus has read it and I haven't. He's 19, speaks Latin fluently, and is a terrible show-off. But my best friend Lizzy sometimes used to sneak me off to her church on Sunday without my Mom finding out, so sometimes I know things that he thinks I won't. Like, for example, the significance of the notice that he posted on all of the public message boards in town.

"Hieronymus Kirkman has kindly bestowed a goat on his beloved son, Germanicus Flavius Kirkman, in order that he may make merry with his friends. All are invited to join in the merriment. RSVP so I don't run out of wine."

This was being read out in a slightly sing-song voice as I entered the coffee shop. A small gaggle of girls from school were standing around near the poster board where my brother's notice was to be found nestled among advertisements for the local Rotary club dinner and a First Nations drum festival.

"That family is like so weird. Who even talks like that?" This was said snottily by a girl whose name I did not know.

The girl who had been reading out the poster turned. My stomach knotted. Cataline O'Hare was still recognizably William's sister beneath the sparkling lipstick and glittery eye shadow. Streaks of artificial blond cut across her otherwise black hair, and there was a kind of vapid emptiness in her eyes. William used to have that look when he stood on the margins of the schoolyard pretending not to

XXVI

care that no one liked him. The lipstick smiled and opened on a luxuriant sigh. "Germanicus," she purred.

Nameless Girl looked alarmed. She had misstepped. Somehow, incomprehensibly, my brother's notice was not meant to be the subject of ridicule. "I, like, thought he was, like, a total loser."

"A hideous dweeb with a massive overbite. I know. Until—" Catty pulled out her cell-phone and began fiddling with the screen. "I bet you've never seen a real-life ugly duckling before." She showed the phone around, "I caught him last week going into the library. I so wish I had the before picture."

The girls gathered round the screen entranced. One of them compared him to some popular boy-toy whose movies or music I wasn't familiar with. Another asked Catty if she could zoom in on his ass. I cringed and started to edge towards the door. Cataline looked up. For a moment I thought that she had seen me, and I could feel the prickles rising on the back of my neck. Such a stupid feeling, to be scared of nothing. *Sticks and stones can break your bones...* The childhood chant hadn't worked then and it didn't help now. I stepped back out into the street trying to look casual, then turned and ran.

"So," I dumped my schoolbooks on the table across from my brother, "Cataline O'Hare thinks you're a dreamboat."

XXVII

"Please don't ever use that language in my presence again." Germanicus appeared to be in the middle of a difficult passage so he crinkled his brow and failed to look up from his book. "Viv," my brother called me by a nickname that only he used. "You ever think about what would have happened if the Athenians had lost at Salamis?"

Salamis was a big naval battle where the Greeks decimated the invading Persian fleet. "I don't know. Probably you'd be studying classical Persian and I'd be named after one of Xerxes' wives."

"Maybe. I always wonder. I mean, Rome owes a lot to Greece, but would the Roman Empire have actually not existed if the Greeks had lost? Or would they just have adopted a different set of cultural influences?"

This was one of those stupid hypothetical questions that all of my older brothers found infinitely interesting. I had nothing to contribute so I scavenged the cupboards for the snack I hadn't been able to have at the coffee shop. I found some leftover chicken with figs and took it to the table. "She's planning to come your party, you know. She's hoping you'll build a gilded podium in the front yard, and then pose on it while she burns incense to your hot bod."

Germanicus looked confused for a moment and then adopted the weird, upturned-eyes expression that he wears when he's scavenging his photographic memory for bits of conversation he only half-caught the first time around. "Oh. You mean Bratty Catty. I'm sure it's a stupid joke."

XXVIII

"You've been away the last three years. You don't know Cataline. She's not the same as she was before William died. She devours boys. Popular boys. Pretty boys. Strong boys. I think one of them was a world-class ping-pong champion."

"I am neither popular nor pretty nor strong, and I am merely adequate at ping-pong."

"You're nineteen years old and you've almost earned your BA. You're smart. She hasn't gobbled up a smart boy yet."

Germanicus looked simultaneously wearied and indifferent. "I'm sure there's a reason for that." He took out his pocket knife and removed some invisible imperfections from the tip of his pencil. "It's probably that smart boys aren't that dumb."

"Catty's not dumb either. And she's evil."

He looked up, stoically accepting that he was going to have to endure more of this conversation. "Viv, listen to me. I don't care if she rises out of our pond stark naked on a clam-shell. Unless she has literally divined the recipe for a love potion that obliterates man's reason, free will and personality, I will remain indifferent. Until I have earned my doctorate I have neither the time nor the inclination to pursue the fairer sex."

I rolled my eyes. "You know what happens to men who think they can spurn a goddess. Venus is listening, you know, and she can't stand to be ignored."

GHOST R⊙AST

The scent of a slowly roasting goat enveloped the front lawn in a beatific cloud of lemony thyme. My mother was in the kitchen whipping up some gourmet nibblies, and Germanicus was stocking the serving table with soda-pop under the delusion that some guests might prefer cola to mead.

A car pulled in at the far end of the drive. The party wasn't supposed to start for another hour, so I was surprised when a slender girl hopped out and blew the driver a kiss good-bye. Did Germanicus have friends I didn't know about? *Girl* friends? It seemed unlikely. I craned to get a better view. A pair of delicate glasses framed her eyes, and a brown dress with a twee watering-can motif fell almost to her ankle. Her hair was brushed back into a French braid with the blond highlights tucked in so you could barely see them. Her make-up was whisper thin. Instead of a purse she carried a bulky hemp bag that clearly contained books. The transformation was so complete I hardly even recognized Catty until she had nearly reached the house.

"Germanicus!" She ran towards my brother and embraced him. He looked stiff and stunned, like he always does when people touch him. "It's been so long!"

"Octavia!" My mother called me up to the house and out of earshot. As mom gave me instructions for how to baste the goat with a bottle of my father's homemade wine I watched Cataline work her magic. Within under a minute, my brother had visibly relaxed. He looked like he might even be conversing in complete sentences. I scowled. The only sound I could make out clearly was Cataline's laughter, melodic and tinkly like clinked glasses. I wondered if she practiced in front of a mirror.

My mom finished giving me instructions and I was left on the porch clutching a bottle of wine while Cataline pulled something out of her bag and showed it to my brother. A sheaf of papers tied with a ribbon. Germanicus didn't reach for it. He only nodded, looking dangerously compliant. Catty glanced towards me for just a moment, then her hand alighted on Germanicus' shoulder and she began to guide him down the path towards the pastures.

XXXI

"Octavia!" My mother's voice was sharper now. "That meat is going to burn!"

I sighed and went over to the fire pit. In the distance, I could hear the sound of the boat-house doors creaking open and the canoe being launched onto the pond. Smart boys weren't that stupid. So how had she managed to get him to go off alone with her in under five minutes?

I tried to shake the thought from my mind as I poured the libations of wine over the slowly roasting victim. I hadn't mentioned it to anyone, but it was six years today, exactly, since William O'Hare had disappeared. I knelt down on the grass on the opposite side of the roasting animal and reached into my pocket. I produced two small cakes made of pressed flour and fine oil. I poured a little wine over each one and placed them on the hot coals beneath the goat, offering them as a sacrifice to Pluto and Persephone in the hopes of winning a better afterlife for my friend.

As the cakes smoked, I sat back against a little tussock of grass and studied the roasting kid. I felt sort of sorry for it: I wouldn't want to spend an entire day spinning in dizzy circles over a hot fire with people occasionally coming by to douse me in my own rendered fats. The goat had no head, but you know how they say that sometimes when a person's hand has been cut off, there is a phantom hand that remains in its place? The goat had a phantom head. It turned it towards me as the smoke of the burning cakes rose up into its nostrils.

"Can you answer me a question?" I asked it quietly.

XXXII

It cocked its head sagely to one side.

"Is he dead? William, I mean...I didn't exactly see him die. Maybe he escaped." I surveyed the head hopefully.

It looked mournful and swayed from side to side in the manner of a goat.

"So he is dead?"

A dark fire came into its eyes and it shook its head more forcefully.

"You mean he isn't dead."

The fiery specter moved again, this time slow and mysterious.

"Do you mean that he is, or that he isn't?"

The goat stopped spinning, nodded very significantly and looked me straight in the eye. I held its gaze, determined to get an answer, but it won the staring contest. I looked away and started poking at the fire. I wished Catullus was there. He would have been able to see the goat's head too, only he would have known what it was trying to tell me. Unfortunately, Catullus was out of the country and my father had never taught me how to read signs and portents properly.

"I miss William," I said. The goat looked sympathetic and we gazed together sadly in the direction of the woods where William had been lost. For a moment I could see myself running up the path to William's house, ten years old, my skirt torn, my hair full of burrs, my shoelaces trailing in the mud. Right away, I'd led William's mother to the exact place where William had been lost, but

XXXIII

the path had not been there. I remembered Mrs. O'Hare, her pink fingernails curling too tight around her cell-phone, telling someone that I had forgotten the way, but I knew that wasn't true. I'd been that way a thousand times before. It wasn't that I'd gotten lost, it was that the path wasn't there.

"I think you forgot something," said a voice that was slow and portentous and that just for a moment seemed to come from the goat. I shook my head, startled, and looked up. It was Germanicus' friend Thomas, our neighbour from across the street.

"Don't do that!" I shouted. "You scared me."

Picking up a stick, Thomas squatted next to the fire and rearranged the coals. His slender face was thoughtful and the firelight made his pale, curly hair look like a burning bush. "I was just going to say that when you're making an offering for the dead you're supposed to face the rising sun. It's a symbol of hope."

I pouted at the fire pit. The goat had courteously hidden its ghost head so as not to scandalize the guest.

"Thomas?"

"Yes?"

"Do you believe me?"

"About what?"

"William. Do you believe that he really fell into a well, and I really saw it happen?"

Thomas considered. "I remember when William disappeared. The twins and I, we made a search of our own.

XXXIV

It was the first time that I ever got to track something important. But we didn't find any well." By the twins he meant my older siblings, Antonia and Catullus.

I frowned and stared at the coals. "So basically, you think I'm lying. Just like everyone else."

"No. Sometimes a man turns into a wolf. He sees as a wolf sees, moves as a wolf moves, and feels the blood of the wolf running in his veins. Yet if another man sees him, he only perceives a man."

I tried to see Thomas as a wolf, but I couldn't get past the fact that he was a slender white boy wearing a bright-green conservation authority t-shirt and faded jeans. "You mean I'm delusional?"

Now it was Thomas' turn to look disappointed. "If you think the spirit world is a delusion, why waste good wine?" He gestured towards my little sacrifice.

"So you do believe me?"

"I believe you told the truth. I don't believe that you told all of it."

I slumped down and rested my chin on my knees. He was right. I'd never said anything about taking secrets out of the world. I'd been vague about how William had fallen in. To be honest, I couldn't properly remember that part myself. "There were things I never told because no one would have believed them. They already thought I was insane."

Thomas nodded. "Yes. There were things we never told for that same reason."

XXXV

"What do you mean?" I sat up straight. "Like what?"

I could see that Thomas was deciding what he wanted to say. "Those are old woods. Full of old spirits. But I think whatever you and William found, it didn't belong there. It came from somewhere else, and those woods were always trying to spit it out. Like when there's a thorn that's too deep in your foot to dig out with a knife, and your body has to isolate it. I think when you couldn't find the well, maybe it was like that. Maybe the forest had closed up the paths to protect itself."

"Thomas!" I punched him in the arm, impatiently. "That's not an answer! What did you see?"

"Nothing. Antonia wore the wolf-skin. She was the one who saw." He shrugged with a self-deprecating smile. "I only got to promise never to tell what I hadn't seen."

I sighed and slumped down again. No way would I ever get a secret out of Antonia – not unless she decided on her own to tell. "Do you think," I asked after a while, "if the forest really did just close the path off there would be a way to cut through? That the well is still there?"

Thomas didn't say anything. He'd closed his eyes and looked like he might be saying a prayer. I lowered my head as well, silently addressing the goat. "If I go back," I asked, "will I be able to find him? Now that I'm older?"

The goat's head looked uncertain and replied, "There is something you will forget."

XXXVI

IS THAT A CANOE IN

YOUR POCKET

It was getting late. The party was winding down, and Germanicus and Catty were still not back. Several girls from school had put in a brief appearance, but had eventually left, disappointed at my brother's absence from his own celebration. Now there were just a couple of townies hanging around, drinking the free booze and listening to country music out of the back of someone's truck.

"Don't worry about your brother," Thomas advised. "He knows what kind of a woman Catty is."

XXXVII

"Then why is he still out?"

"There's a good reason, I'm sure." I must have looked skeptical, because Thomas continued. "Once, when we were in elementary school, Catty proposed to marry him. He turned her down."

"Really?" I couldn't imagine it. Yeah, Germanicus was pretty cute now – but that was only because he'd had a childhood overbite so severe that it required medical correction. His enviable jaw was the product of plastic surgery. As a kid, he'd mostly looked like a large-mouth bass.

"She had no intention of marrying him of course. It was a ruse. The idea was that Catty would propose to the biggest nerd in school and Brent would propose to the fat girl. Then, when they showed up, a marriage would be celebrated in which both would be humiliated in front of everyone. Of course Germanicus refused, so I was subbed in as the second biggest nerd."

"See!" I clenched my fists and looked out towards the pond. The moonlight was flickering on the edge of the water, but the island was hidden from view by a curtain of pines. "I warned him that she was evil."

"Actually, I'm grateful for the experience. Before that day, I only saw that Catty was pretty and Susie was fat. Afterwards, I saw that Catty was cruel and Susie was kind. She made a very good wife until her family moved away." Thomas smiled.

I glowered at the moonlight. "Why do the pretty girls have to be so stupid?"

"Not all of them are... But I'll embarrass us both if I say that you're an exception to the rule." His expression continued to look slightly sardonic and vaguely enigmatic, but I thought I caught a touch of red rising towards his ears.

It was hard to tell. Pale boys blush so easily.

I was trying to develop a suitable reply to his compliment when the quiet was disturbed by a loud splash and an ungodly scream.

Everyone was down by the waterside in minutes. Flashlights searched out the dark surface of the water, and beams glinted on the backs of lily-pads. Eventually a human-like form rose from the pool of algae with a screaming damsel in its arms. I so needed a camera. Germanicus would have gotten a serious kick out of seeing himself as the monster in a B-horror-movie.

Catty had stopped shrieking by the time that Germanicus deposited her on the dock, but she still shiverred and would not stop clinging to his shirt. Someone thought to turn on the boathouse lights, and as the illumination flooded over her she started to scream again. Her legs were covered in tiny, jewel-like leeches. There were even a couple on her arms and one big pulsing one, obscenely nestled into the hollow of her throat. She kicked her bare heels frantically against the boards screaming "Get them off!" "Germanicus!!" "Ew! Eww! Eeeeek!" and so on.

XXXIX

Thomas turned to me with a hint of a smile. "I suppose you had better go up to the house and fetch salt. Be very quick. Do not take your time." The sarcasm was whisper thin but I was sure I wasn't imagining it. I nodded, and headed for the kitchen at a leisurely pace.

"Actually, it turns out the ancient physicians were not stupid. Apparently, leeches secrete something into the bloodstream that prevents clotting. They've actually started using them again in modern hospitals. If someone cuts off their finger and it has to be reattached, for example." Germanicus was sitting on the edge of the dock giving an impromptu lecture on the history of leech-craft as he tore the creatures off his skin like used band-aids. Thin streams of blood flowed over his arms and his ankles and he took unholy delight in squashing the leeches against the dock-side before dropping their gelatinous husks back into the pond.

"That's so gross," said one of the townies, a gangling, sallow-faced boy whose name I thought might begin with T.

Catty, to my immense surprise, had calmed down completely. "It's true," she said, studying one of the creatures that had attached itself to her ankle. "They use them in plastic surgery." She turned towards my brother, " You know, it's crazy how we think we're so much smarter than our forefathers, and then we find out that they were right all along." She snaked out a hand across my brother's shoulders, "You missed one, here. You want me to get it for you?"

XL

Germanicus had stopped talking. He was staring at her like a charmed snake. "Uh, yeah. Sure. Thanks."

"This works better," I stepped forward and poured a handful of salt over my brother's head before dropping the container stormily onto the dock. T took advantage of the opportunity to helpfully spread the contents over Cataline's legs and look up her skirt. Germanicus gave me his 'does not compute' look as though my anger were less than entirely just.

Catty seized the initiative. She brushed the salted leeches from her legs and stood up, reaching down to take Germanicus' hand. "Don't you have an outdoor shower? Over by the bunk-house?"

"We do."

I surreptitiously kicked him, hoping to reboot whatever faulty process was making him think *that* might be a good idea.

"But actually," he corrected himself, "the water's really cold. You could use the one up at the house. I'm sure mom will give you a towel. And maybe you can borrow some of Antonia's old clothes."

She smiled, and I could see that she knew exactly how well she was pulling off the muddy-survivor-in-a-soaking-wet-dress look. As soon as she was gone I moved to loom over Germanicus like a Fury.

"Well," he said. "I think that went okay."

"Okay? You were gone for hours! You lost the boat! You..." I didn't know even what to accuse him of.

XLI

"Oh, well that was on purpose," he shrugged as if he had been entirely in control of everything the whole time. "She tried to kiss me, so I capsized the canoe." He stood up and brushed himself off.

Thomas cleared his throat. "I think the shower Catty suggested would be a good idea. I'll come with you. Someone's going to have to make sure you don't have leeches in places you can't see."

Germanicus showered in his clothes, then disappeared with Thomas into the bunkhouse. I followed at a distance. The bunkhouse is the private domain of the Kirkman boys, and my brothers have guaranteed grotesque punishments to any girl who would dare invade its precincts.

But I knew a secret. Antonia had discovered it years ago: a place in back where you can crawl in behind the peonies. There's a vent there, and Antonia had taught me that if you're super quiet, you can just lie in the greenery and listen to all the boy's plans. It was how she'd always had dirt on them in case they ever tried to cross her. I wasn't supposed to use it except in emergencies. Like now.

As I wriggled into place I could hear Thomas talking. "It's an amusing image. Catty with a tongue like a chameleon springing out to kiss you from the far side of the canoe. But it obviously did not happen like that."

Germanicus paused. "Well...she did try to kiss me. And I did capsize the canoe. But I might have implied a

XLII

more direct temporal and causal relationship between those two events than is, in fact, the case."

"Mmmm. It may be."

"All right. Let's say, for the sake of argument, that I let Catty kiss me. First, if word got around it would completely destroy my Stoic cred. Second, Viv would kill me. She hates Catty's guts."

"Yes. She seems very invested."

"Octavia thinks that Catty believes that whatever happened to William is her fault. You know how girls are. Instant drama, just add estrogen." I could hear Germanicus' shoulder bone pop as he shrugged. I hoped it hurt.

"All right. Let's say, for the sake of argument, that 'stoic cred' is...a thing. Why did you go with her in the first place?

"Catty said today is the anniversary of William's disappearance. She had a little bundle of papers that she wanted to take to the island to leave as a memorial. Apparently that was William's favourite place. How could I have said no?"

"You couldn't. That was clever of her."

"Yeah, I know! She's smarter than I thought she'd be." Pause. "Not that she's a threat." Prolonged pause. "Don't look at me like that!"

"You were gone somewhat longer than a moment of silence."

"Somehow we got into a philosophical discussion."

"Somehow."

"Look, can I get dressed yet? It's getting cold."

"It will affect your Stoic Cred." I heard a faint sucking, ripping sound. "That's the last one. You are now declared leech-free and sorely in need of a bath."

There was a rustle of cloth as my brother pulled dry clothes onto wet limbs. "Alright. I'm off." The door of the bunkhouse swung open, clattered closed.

When Thomas could no longer hear the sound of Germanicus' footsteps he said, "Okay Octavia, you can come out now."

PATRIA POTESTAS

I stood in the front hall, hands clasped in front of me, waiting. My mother was bent in a posture of prayer before the little altar where dwelt the household gods. There are two of them. One is a hefty mass-market statue of the Buddha, fat-bellied, red and smiling. It came to live with us after the death of my paternal grandfather. At that time our home was bereft of ancestral deities so Julia had rescued the laughing statue from Grandpa's cottage and insisted we install it as patron of our realm.

The other is a strange, thin-faced god with a crest of blue hair and an intense otherworldly gaze. Catullus encountered it in a vision when he was about my age and drew it in oil pastel. Since nobody had the skill to make a three-dimensional representation, the *lar* remained trapped on paper, locked behind a pane of glass in a thick wooden frame. Although we were careful to leave offerings for it on a regular basis, I think everyone was a little afraid of it. For that reason, my mother prayed to the red Buddha, a curl of smoke rising from a stick of incense in front of her as she asked the *lares* to ensure that her children and her lands would remain safe while she was gone.

Germanicus arrived at my side smelling of lemon-scented dish soap and adopted his own suitably pious posture. A couple of minutes later my mother looked up and nodded at us. We approached in turn, kissed her cheek, and bid her farewell. She picked up her tapestry bag, her long fingers whitening as they tightened around the opalescent handle. "And you won't forget to garland the wells for *Fontinalia*?" My mother's list of things Germanicus mustn't forget while she was away had absorbed the better part of his morning. He'd already reassured her about this particular detail several times.

"I won't forget. I promise."

She didn't look convinced, not because she didn't trust Germanicus but because she was leaving the house – something she almost never did – and because she sincerely feared that the hubris of air travel offended the gods. She smoothed back her dark, plaited hair and strained a smile. My father appeared at the door, dressed in his tweed, a

XLVI

fringe of grey-white hair sticking out from under the edges of his fedora. He nodded to my brother and me, and said simply, "*Vale.*"

"*Vale, pater,*" we replied in unison, each with a slight bow. My father reached into his briefcase and produced a slightly flattened pinwheel. It was the old fashioned kind with a metal pin and wooden stem; a relic from his childhood that served as the symbol of dad's *patria potestas,* his authority as the father of the house. He handed it to Germanicus wordlessly, but with a look that made it clear what he expected.

A minute later we were standing on the step in front of the house and waving them off. The car wound out of sight and the sound of tires crunching on gravel slowly faded. For the next two weeks Germanicus and I would be home, alone.

I looked up at my brother. "So, now that we're free, what do you want to do?"

My query had clearly produced some kind of error message in his brain. "First," he said slowly, "I promised Dad I'd rescue his canoe. Second, I have a thesis to write. I'm pretty sure you're supposed to go practice your lyre." He was already pulling on a pair of old hip-waders, and before I could explain the concept of "fun" to him, he was gone.

I went back inside. Apart from the refrigerator, and the usual creaks and groans that troubled its hundred-year-old skeleton, the house was silent. I took down my lyre from the shelf above the fireplace and plucked absently at the strings. I wanted to compose a hymn to honour William, but everything I played just sounded like a jumble of sad notes. Staring listlessly out of the window, I wondered what had been in those papers that Cataline had left on the island.

It had taken a couple of weeks for the police to finally close the search for William. I remembered how Catty had been then. Every day I'd seen her in the halls at school, laughing and talking with her friends as though nothing of import was going on. From time to time she would see me, and then there would be a flash of dark fire in her eyes before she closed them, very deliberately, and looked away as though my existence were something that needed to be erased. Sometimes she would say something about the "girl who cried 'Well'," but mostly she didn't interact with me except to make sure that rumours slowly spread behind my back.

Making my life hell had been the only way that Catty showed any kind of feeling about her brother's disappearance. When they had finally given up and put in a memorial stone, down in the corner of the graveyard by the lake, Catty wore a little black hat with a veil of fine mesh to hide her face – but you could tell that what she was hiding was boredom, not grief.

No way did I believe she was grieving now.

I heard the door open, and plucked a quick arpegio so that Germanicus would think I was doing my work. He went straight upstairs and I heard his bedroom door close.

XLVIII

Behind that door was a room piled almost to the ceiling with books, and once I lost Germanicus to it he might not emerge for days. I craned my neck back to stretch, returned the lyre to its shelf and paced through the empty rooms, looking in vain for something to tidy or polish. Mother had left everything in a state of perfection.

Once I was confident that my brother was sunk nose deep in his books, I snuck down to the waterside. The canoe lay on the bank covered in slimy algae and trailing weeds like dryad's hair.

The grey sky brought out the rusty tones in the dark rock of the island and made the Folly look abandoned and forlorn. I don't know which of my siblings gave it that name but there was nothing better that it could have been called. I suppose it had been the kingdom of our childhood, representing the dreams of all the Kirkman kids. There was a crumbling palisade wall, with sharpened timbers leaning out at different angles like broken teeth. A stone altar had been erected within the half-built walls of a cob house. A series of old, blue-green bottles hung from one of the trees, each one containing a little scene painstakingly painted onto the inside. Vines and grasses were growing up over most of it, and the rain had lent a cloudy patina to the glass.

Cataline's offering was on the altar. I went over and picked it up: a sheaf of papers, heavy cream-coloured, stock. They were bound together with a pale pink ribbon. I opened it gingerly.

XLIX

The pages were blank. It felt like sacrilege, desecration, to have left such a meaningless gift in this place. I went through them again, almost unable to believe that such callowness was even possible. Her "memorial" really had been nothing more than a ruse to get Germanicus to come out here with her alone.

My hatred for her germinated as I paddled back to shore. It put down roots as I went out and did my garden chores, plucking ugly, fat-bodied slugs off of the cabbage plants. It grew as I sat looking at the telephone, trying to think of people I could invite over, remembering the names of old friends who hadn't spoken to me in years. It flowered as I sat alone at the dinner table picking at a plate of overcooked noodles that I had made for myself. As night fell Germanicus finally came down. He waved to me with a casual smile, and then headed out to do his chores without a word. The only thing he said when he came in was, "Good night," before disappearing again into his lair.

I walked into the games room searching for some way to occupy myself. Darts. Old pinball machines. A neat shelf of jigsaw puzzles. I took one down and tried to take an interest in it, but my eyes kept drifting towards the window.

Outside the moon was rising, a swollen red circle above the dark ragged silhouette of the forest. I had promised not to go there, not ever again. I reached into my pocket and stroked the surface of the stone that William had sent me. My promise to William was older. It came first.

THE FOREST

SWALLOWS TIME

Dear William,

I have a secret, and I can't tell anyone what it is. It's killing me. This is a really big secret: most secrets are petty. It's not that they're really terrible. It's usually not like, "when I was a young woman back in China I drowned my newborn son in the bathtub." Most secrets are like, "Remember how someone posted those photos of you on the workplace computers, and it meant that you didn't get the promotion? That was me. It was because you never noticed that I liked you." Or "I killed a squirrel out in the back woods, just so that I could know what it was like to have

LI

something die in my hands. When I found it, it had a broken leg. It bit me. I cut it open from the crotch to the nape and watched it rolling around on the ground. I kind of liked it at the time, but now I'm so afraid of myself that I feel guilty if I squash a spider."

Actually, those are pretty good as secrets go. A lot of the time it's like, "I first slept with a boy when I was thirteen. It was because I was really lonely and I wanted to prove that someone liked me. He never talked to me again." Sometimes it's "I spit in the soup at work because I hate the customers." Go on the internet some time: it's absolutely swimming with this stuff. Stupid, petty, dumb secrets that don't count. Secrets that are shameful just because they're not even worth having.

I wonder if a lot of your secrets were like that. If they were things that just weighed on you and weighed on you because they were totally disproportionate in their weight. Secrets like, "I pick my nose and then roll it around between my fingers. I like it when there's a really big hard piece in the middle and the rest is sticky." Somehow I think that they weren't, but I don't remember.

Here's my big secret. I'm lonely, and I miss you. That's not a secret, it's just cheesy crap, but you know it's true. Do you think I'll get to see you again when I rescue you?

Love Octavia

I wrote this letter on one of the blank pieces of stock that Catty had left on the island. Slowly, reverently, I placed a sprig of rue in its centre, for remembrance, then rolled it up. I was building a ritual, and this was its final component. I added it to my backpack. Next to the note, on my desk, sat an old, grey shoe-box. *Octavia,* it was labeled in my mother's hand, *10 Years Old.* Our attic contained dozens of boxes just like these. This was the one from the year William went away.

I replaced all of the treasures that I wasn't going to need and then tucked the box away under my bed. I'd put it away properly later. Outside, behind the back pasture, the first amber sunlight was just starting to filter in through the broad-limbed pines that rose above the forest. I shouldered my backpack and headed out.

An old gate hung on rusted hinges at the back of the pasture. Several faded pieces of ribbon clung to the wire of the fence – all that remained of garlands that Antonia had hung there over the years. I remembered her and Catullus coming to me in the night, dressed in their Roman finery, their faces grave. They had brought me out here, marked the threshold between our property and the woods with an offering of honey and wine, and then exhorted me never to cross this line again. I had been small then, and they had seemed so serious and adult, but the truth was they were only a little older than I am now.

I had brought with me honey and wine so that the gods of the forest would forgive my trespass. I poured it out on the path, and pushed on the gate. It should have been a smooth, priestly action, the gate yeilding before me, but actually it was so long since it had opened that it was all matted with grasses and wild grape vines. I pushed on it as hard as I could, but it wouldn't budge. Gathering my dignity and my skirts, I clambered over the fence.

It was six years since I had last been down this path, yet I could remember the little mossy outcroppings of stone, the rainwater creek that cut across the path, the fortress that my brothers had built on its banks in one of their countless campaigns against the Parthians, the massive pine tree with vast knots of resin that dripped down like honeyed candle wax.

I walked. The weather was unseasonably clement, and it seemed as though every mossy hollow had preserved some lingering breath of dying summer. Finally, around noon, I heard the sound of water trickling over mossy stone. The dense foliage gave way to a hill-side down which sprang a bright, leeping cataract of crystal water. The fairy falls, William had always called them, and I had imagined nymphs playing in the spray. I picked my way up over rocks slippery with lime-green algae until I reached the headwaters.

A flat rock interrupted the spring's flow. I perched on it and wove a wreath from wildflowers that I had collected along the way: native species, which I hoped would please the god of the spring. I called him Fontus, for this was what the Romans called all of the gods of all of the wells and fountains in the world. This one seemed benevolant, laughing, but you never can tell with gods. Sometimes their laughter is at man's expense.

When I had finished my work, I slipped off my hoodie and skirt. Underneath, I wore a bathing suit: two piece, shimmering blue, in a style that my mother would have forbidden. Antonia had taken me to the beach once, and had bought it for me so that I could have the experience of being beautiful, young and unashamed. Mostly I'd just felt exposed, and I hadn't taken off my shirt except to go in the water.

But today there were no boys to see me, only the forest. I could risk being beautiful and unashamed as I lowered myself to kneel in the crisp-cold stream.

"Fontus," I prayed, "native river spirit, whose waters give life to these woods. I come to you as a suppliant, seeking refuge for a heart that has been wearied long with grief. I ask you to look kindly on my offerings," I placed the wreath on the earth above the gurgling spring, my teeth chattering in the late September air, "and to intercede for me with the spirits of this wood so that the path, long hidden, will be made clear again." On the water, I placed a little boat, a toy that William had left by accident on our island. It was made of cedar, with a paper sail. In it, I placed the letter that I had written to William and a little votive offering of grain.

It bobbed unsteadily over the churning waters of the stream until about halfway down it capsized. My soggy letter ran with tears of ink as the little boat disappeared beneath the waves.

That was when I noticed the eyes watching me from the woods.

With a small scream, I grabbed my hoodie and covered my chest. The figure peered at me from the underbrush. It was only a child. Small, almost skeletal, dressed practically in rags. I didn't think that he could be more than seven years old. My first thought was that he was playing pirates, but the hunger in his eyes was too real for a game. He said something to me in French which I mostly didn't understand. There was, however, one word that stood out: "William."

I dressed hurriedly and followed as he scrambled ahead of me down the hill.

W.W.M.A.D

The sun had just passed overhead and the air was pregnant with its heat. I had arrived at a cul de sac criss-crossed with the skidding tire-marks of dirt-bikes. The way was blocked by a small rock-face, about twelve or thirteen feet high, made up of blocky limestone boulders that had been carried here millennia ago on the shoulders of a glacier. Time had sucked them down into the dark earth.

I began to climb. It was not difficult: there were plenty of hand-holds and the face was not quite shear. I had nearly reached the top when I put my weight down on a mossy patch and my foot went through. My leg went in as far as the knee, twisted, and then a blackening pain overcame me.

As the world slowly reemerged from the blackness, I became aware that my leg was stuck in a deep crevice. When I tried to ease it out a shrill pang ran up into my hip. If my ankle wasn't broken, it was badly twisted. I lacked the fortitude to pull it out.

I hooked my backpack on a small root that jutted out from the edge of the cliff face. I was nearly at the top, maddeningly close to flat ground, and I hoped that my salvation lay in some unused pocket. Perhaps I had brought along an old walkie-talkie that would miraculously connect me with my brother, or a hypodermic needle filled with local anesthetic, or an Atlantean crystal with the ability to magically knit together shattered bone. The most useful thing that I found was a small, neon green whistle that I once won in a potato-shoot at the local fair. I unclipped it, my hands shaking and unsteady, and put it to my lips. Instead of a high, shrill, urgent summons, there came a quiet, rattling, reedy bleat. I tried again. I closed my eyes and cleared my mind in concentration. I took air into my lungs. I let it out. I breathed. I focused on the breathing. I became breath. The whistle let out a thin and desperate squeak, then slipped from my fingers and fell into a bush seven feet below. I felt sick.

"William," I whispered to the not-there ghost. "This is why you are never to play with sorcery." I slumped against the rock face feeling lost. "I asked to be taken to where you are. It never occurred to me that where you are might just be dead."

"Oh no," William's voice was nowhere, chiding. "Our situations are completely different. You still have light. And you might be rescued."

I tried to take comfort in this, but I remembered my promise to William, that I would go get help. I imagined him, waiting in the darkness for help that never came, and I started to be afraid.

I looked down at my wrist where I wore a woven bracelet made for me by my sister Antonia. On it were the letters WWMAD which stood for "What Would Marcus Aurelius Do?" Marcus Aurelius was a Roman Emperor and a Stoic, which was potentially helpful in a situation like mine. I set my face like a marble statue, an icon of Roman virtue, and tried to extricate the injured ankle from the crevice.

After what seemed like an eternity, I managed to get it free. My ankle was black and swollen, bent at an unnatural angle. Putting weight on it was impossible, but I managed to pull myself up to the flat ground using only my remaining limbs.

I lay on the ground, gasping and staring at the sky. The timeless dark had deepened as if a storm were coming or twilight had sneaked up on me unexpected. I turned my head, and knew where I was. Just a few short feet down a winding stretch of path was the hollow tree where William and I used to turn off to find the Well. When I had come here with the police there had been only brambles and thorns growing, but now it was as it had been. The path that led to the Well was here, just as I remembered it.

Dragging my leg along behind me like a black balloon I struggled towards the path.

CAPTAIN OBLIVIOUS

Germanicus' first day as interim ruler of the Kirkman kingdom had been a good one. He tidied the lawn, rescued the canoe, and spent about fifteen minutes surveying his realm to make sure the animals were all happy and in their proper places. Finding that all was in order, he retired to his chambers. He changed into clean clothes and then read three chapters of Augustine's Confessions, half of a horror novel, and an essay about how barbarian languages had influenced the development of Latin during late antiquity. He then wrote 3000 words of his thesis, about 800 of which would likely be deemed worthy of potential inclusion.

There was a picky point concerning the fourth century Catholic-Arian conflict that he wanted clarified, so he fired off an e-mail to Fr. Xu. The priest had been a friend of Dad's back when he was teaching Latin at a private Catholic school. When Germanicus had managed to get himself into university at the tender age of sixteen, my father had recruited the priest to make sure that his son remembered to perform basic human functions like bathing and eating. Writing the e-mail reminded Germanicus that eating was on Mom's list of things that he was supposed to do while she was away, so he had a grapefruit. Then he did some more reading. When the clock struck seven he went downstairs and did the chores. He said goodnight to me, washed the dishes and considered making supper, but opted to eat another grapefruit instead. Noting that I looked miserable, he thoughtfully didn't chide me for having failed to bring the laundry in.

Since he hadn't gotten very much done on his schoolwork he only let himself watch one episode of HBO's Rome. He played it at +30% normal speed, and tried to skip over the worst of the smut. While watching he dipped into his secret stash of chocolate-flavoured energy bars. Since he considered them a guilty pleasure, he kept them hidden inside the old dumbwaiter that run up to his room.

The senses having been sufficiently indulged, he got back to business. At 11:30 he made sure I'd gone to bed. My door was closed. I wasn't downstairs. Good enough.

Day two. Germanicus gets up, showers, eats a grapefruit and leaves the house at 6am to drive to Kingston. As I am heading out to the woods, he attends his first class. He spends the rest of the morning napping at the library with a copy of Gibbons' Decline and Fall. As I bathe my feet in the fairy springs, he splurges on a fancy yogurt and granola thing for lunch. Next, he attends his afternoon classes and then, unaware that I am at that very moment sinking my ankle into a hole in an ancient rock-face, he runs into a friend of his: Sheila.

Sheila is taking Latin, even though she knows nothing about the language, mostly so that she will have an excuse to demand that Germanicus edit her compositions. In fairness, Germanicus is likewise signed up for English mostly so that he will have a reason to make her explain poetry to him. They've been studying each others respective subjects for three years now. Naturally, they have never gone out and Germanicus denies any romantic interest. She detains him well into the evening feigning confusion about conjugating irregular verbs in the pluperfect and ranting about her boyfriend problems. Around six, he calls to tell me that he'll be late but I don't pick up.

He finally arrives home shortly after 11. As he comes around the sharpest of the driveway's many turns, the headlights suddenly illuminate a pale, placid face. Slamming on the brakes, he veers hard to the left. There's a hideous scraping sound and the car jolts to a stop in the midst of my father's blueberry bushes. Shaken, Germanicus jerks the transmission into reverse as though a speedy retreat will somehow undo the damage that has already been done. He parks, climbs out and glares at the goat who is still standing in the dead middle of the drive. It stares defiantly back at him and continues to chew on the greens that it has purloined from the garden.

In the merciless glare of the headlights, Germanicus inspects the blueberries. The patch is scarred by deep, tire-shaped ruts and the roots of several bushes have been exposed. He takes a moment to set things right, straightening the lopsided plants and spreading the mulch around until everything looks tidy again. This is when he notices that the laundry is still hanging on the line. After the goat is wrangled back to its pasture, and the braying horde of its brethren are fed their suppers, he takes down the laundry and folds it. A quick survey of the garden reveals that the delinquent goat has nibbled on four cabbages and consumed most of a kale plant. Germanicus reprimands himself for having failed to tell me that if he gets home late, the goats must be fed at 7.

Inside, he is relieved to find that I haven't left any dirty dishes and the house appears to be in order. Isis, the cat, sidles around his legs, whining for more food. Antonia named it after the Egyptian deity, but Germanicus always thinks of it as being named for the terrorist organization. He kicks it on his way into the kitchen.

He consumes a can of chick-peas, a raw zucchini, some milk, and an oatmeal cookie. This is so that he can in honesty claim that all four food groups were covered. Next, he checks the messages: one from my school, skip, another from Cataline, SKIP. He listens in full to the one from my father, which translated into English is, "I want to assure you that we have arrived."

Since the day has been long, he treats himself to a root-beer and ouzo, then softly knocks on my bedroom door. "Hey, Viv, I'm home. You want to come watch a movie?" No answer. Probably, I'm asleep. So he writes me a note that reminds me to put the laundry away in the morning and slips it under my door.

It is not a note that I will ever read.

SOMETHING

IMPORTANT

When I tired of crawling, I searched the underbrush for a stick that I could use as a crutch. Before, when I had come here with William, the path that led to the Well had seemed quite ordinary but now the clouds seemed pregnant with unspent thunder and the air buzzed with a strange, half-heard trill. I felt as though someone were walking alongside me but whenever I turned my head there was nobody there. "Nerves," I told myself. "It's only nerves."

"What are you nervous about?"

I started and turned. He wasn't there, not exactly, but I could see the place where he would have been standing and knew the expression on his face. No, the face was different than it had been. He was older, but still had the same stern look of stubborn refusal to allow the world to tell him lies. He took a step towards me. I felt an uneasy feeling, like when you know that someone has entered your personal space but they're standing in your blind spot.

"Do you remember?" he asked. He was wearing a long coat. I could feel its hem brushing against the back of my leg as he moved to stand beside me.

"I remember." I reached into my pocket and pulled out the secret. We had come here on the day that he died and locked a secret in this stone. I remembered William handing me a folded sheet of tracing paper. A much older child's handwriting had been copied onto it in a slightly shaky hand.

"What is this?" I asked. It was written in big loopy cursive. I wasn't very good at reading cursive.

"It's Catty's. I'm going to put it in the Well and then it will be gone out of the world." There was something wrong with the way that he said this. He looked the same as he looked that one time we had burned up an anthill with a magnifying glass: not really malicious, but with a sort of unwholesome curiosity.

"Is it a bad secret?"

"No. It's a good secret. That's why I'm going to take it away from her, because she doesn't deserve it." His lip crinkled and for just a moment the muscles in his cheek tugged at his eye and made it all go mean.

"Germanicus says that Catty is a little Messalina."

"What does that mean."

"Messalina was the Emperor Claudius' wife. She was very evil."

"What did she do?"

I shrugged. "They say that I'm too young to know. But you have to tell me what Catty did."

William didn't say anything. He looked at the ground for a second, and then, having studied the underbrush he picked up a stone. It was grey, ordinary and nearly smooth, but with lines here and there like when you try to flatten out a candy-wrapper but your fingernail always leaves a crease. He read Catty's secret, which was really just some stupid stuff about a boy she had a crush on. Then he put the stone into his mouth and handed it to me. "This is today's secret," he said.

I popped it in my mouth and twirled it around like a lollipop or hard candy. It occurred to me, I don't know why, that I could keep it there, in my mouth. "I'm not giving it back," I said. "I'm going to keep this one. The Well can have the others." I stowed the stone in my cheek.

William scowled. "You'll ruin everything." He went over to the edge of the Well and looked down, "Vivi, the water is there at the bottom of the Well. The last time that we dropped a secret in, the Well was dry. Do you suppose that there is a spring down there?"

"Probably," I said, "it is the spring of eternal youth. Like the alchemists used to look for."

"What's an alchemist?"

"It's like a magician, only they used all kinds of metals and things like that. They were looking for the Philosopher's Stone and eternal life and how to turn base metals into gold."

"What does it mean for a metal to be base?"

"I think it means that the metals come from very deep in the world. Like the base of a column."

William nodded. "Do you think that if we had some deep metals from the columns of the world that they would turn into gold if we dropped them into the spring?"

"I don't know. We would have to dig up some of the right kind of metal to try it out."

William had, it seemed, forgotten about the secret. I moved the stone from my mouth into my pocket. I would tease him with it later, and then we would throw it in the Well. We got down on our hands and knees and began to dig. We could go down quite a long way in some places, but in others you hit limestone almost immediately. After a long time, we found something. William reached in and pulled it up. It already shone, almost like gold, but I thought that it was probably a kind of quartz.

"Is this a base metal?" he asked.

"Yes." I was playing make-believe.

LXIX

"Then I will see if it turns into gold in the spring." He went over to the side of the Well and said, "I will need something to hang on to."

"What do you mean?" I said.

"To go down. I have to be able to hold on to the stone. Otherwise, how will I know whether it turned into gold or not?"

"You can't, don't be an idiot."

"I'm not an idiot, Vivi," he said. "If this is the fountain of eternal youth then I will have found something of great value. I will be able to bring it back and give it to the whole world. I will have cured death. This is very important."

"I was only making it up," I said. "Just a game. I wasn't serious. I don't even think that is a base metal in your hand."

He looked down at his treasure, crushed. "This isn't a game, Vivi. To do something important, to change the world. It isn't a game."

"William, we're not even ten years old. We have lots of time to do something important."

William's gaze moved through me without becoming less intent. He didn't answer. He knew that he did not have lots of time.

A VERY EVIL

THING TO DO

A slight drizzle of rain spattered the backs of the stones surrounding the Well and cast a golden halo around the rising moon. I didn't recall it becoming night. I slumped down wearily on a fallen birch, trying to rest my leg. Past and present were running together like watery paint. William perched on the edge of the Well, peering in.

Suddenly, he seized hold of a mass of wild grapevines thaat were growing over the masonry. He was already on his belly, wriggling down into the darkness, when I struggled to my feet.

"What are you doing?" I yelled.

He looked up at me, over the ridge of stone. "Something important." And he disappeared.

I stumbled over to the edge of the Well. His fingers were still clinging to the vines but the wine-dark bark had sloughed off and the green wood beneath was slippery with sap. His grip wouldn't last for long. "William, you idiot," I yelled. I grabbed him by the arm and tried to yank him back up. I was sweating and puffing and suddenly, the moon had grown very bright, its halo gone, and now it looked cruelly down. I could barely stand, much less endure the sort of effort needed to pull a boy out of a well. William was a dead weight, not trying to climb, not struggling, not trying to help.

Drops of rain and sweat ran down my arms. I tried to brace myself, to get a better grip. I pitched forward. Grasped at air. Pain cracked like thunder through my leg and I blacked out.

The world swayed and I felt sea-sick, suspended between earth and sky. Sharp vines were cutting into my fingers and when I looked up I realized that somehow, in that moment, I had taken William's place.

He stood above me, at the top of the Well, looking down. His little hands were holding on to mine, but calmly, without any particular effort, and he wasn't trying to pull me up.

"What are you doing? Help me!"

"I will go to the town, I will call everyone to come and make a search. I will leave you alone until I get back." He let go.

I fell, and after what seemed like a little too long, I landed in a puddle of water. There was a loud and distant sounding crack followed by a brief spike of pain before I passed out. When I opened my eyes there was dark. I could just make out a little patch of starlight above. I started to cry. "It wasn't like that...I tried to pull you up. You were too heavy. I wasn't strong enough."

No answer. The water was sucking in and out very slowly, like saliva at the back of the mouth. It was cold and slightly oily. My leg was no longer hurting – a very bad sign because it meant that I was probably in shock.

"William?" I asked the darkness. I could hear a soft dripping, and felt the water level rise.

"Yes," the voice that spoke to me now was softer, quieter. The note of accusation was entirely gone. "It wasn't your fault, Vivi. I know that you tried to save me. You tried to get me out. You tried to go get the old man with the ladder."

I laughed a little, and that made me realize that I was crying and also shivering. The laugh shook in my ribs painfully. "But you said..."

"Vivi, be sensible. How could I have said anything? I've been dead for long time, you know."

"No one knows that for sure. No one knows for sure that you're dead. It's just that you were lost. The place where you disappeared doesn't exist. You must remember, it used to be very simple to find – there was the place with the hollow tree, the one that you could climb up inside and hide, and there was a little ragged hole in the side so that you could look out and watch the people passing by but they couldn't see you. Sometimes you would make a sound like a ghost in there to scare someone. Remember how you scared Catty that one time when she was walking her puppy?"

"Yes, of course I remember that. Do you remember how I tried to poison Catty's puppy?"

"No," I felt suddenly very cold.

"Try to recall. There were some berries that we found out in the forest. You showed them to me. You said that they were deadly nightshade. I took some home and I crushed them up and put them in the dog's dish. It was a very evil thing to do, but I was angry because it was Catty's dog not mine. She only asked once. I had been asking for years and years, every Christmas, every birthday. I told mom and dad that I wanted a dog and there were always reasons why they couldn't. It was too expensive. It was too much work. And then Catty asked once and they went out right away and bought her a puppy. It wasn't even a special occasion. Do you remember this?"

"No," I was really shivering now.

"No. But if you reach down into the water you will find it. Try."

I put my hand down into the muck. There were things wriggling around in there and I felt suddenly sick.

My fingers closed around something dark and smooth. I pulled it up. It was a stone.

"That was one of my secrets, Vivi. One of the secrets that you helped me seal up. We threw it down here, and you never remembered it after that."

I was suddenly angry with him. "Why would you make me a part of something like that?"

"I'm sorry. I never meant to implicate you. It's just that those secrets hurt so much to carry, Vivi. You were the only one who could make them go away."

"And what about now?" I demanded. "Am I here to seal up your last secret with my death?"

"Oh no, it's not like that at all. You see, the Well really was the fountain of youth. Anyone who comes into these waters will never grow old or die. But it is down here at the bottom of a great abyss. And it is very dark, and very lonely."

THOMAS AMONG

THE HURONS

Thomas couldn't sleep on account of being tormented by a deceptively simple problem. Mary Kirkman was going to be out of the country for exactly two weeks. Mary Kirkman was a known obstacle to any romantic designs that a boy might have towards her teenage daughters. This meant that there was a window of exactly two weeks in which to communicate to me the nature and depth of his affections. Only one thing still stood in his way: his best friend.

I will give examples. On the night that Germanicus dunked Catty in the pond, Thomas had been building courage to ask me on a date. Well, not quite a date. More like a casual outing to the small museum where he worked. There was an exhibit of indigenous artifacts visiting from St. Marie among the Hurons, and Thomas had put together a presentation on shamanistic traditions for the local schoolchildren. He was proud of it in a modest way, and he had been trying to find the right moment to suggest that maybe, if I wasn't busy, I would be interested in attending...when Germanicus interrupted his plans by plunging Cataline into a leech-infested swamp.

After his presentation the next day, he came by our house. For half an hour he paced up and down at the end of the driveway trying to think of a reason why he had come to see me. Perhaps he needed to borrow an egg? No. That was stupid. There was no way to turn borrowing an egg into a romantic intrigue. Maybe if you were Casanova. Thomas was not. He sat down on the old stump at the end of the driveway and put his chin on the palm of his hand. As he was sitting there he heard the call of a very rare bird, one that was not often seen in this part of Ontario. Filled with joy, he rushed towards our house. He would claim to have been following the bird call all the way from his house across the street, and offer me this once-in-a-lifetime opportunity to see a white-winged dove.

"Hi Thomas." It was Germanicus. Out doing chores in the yard. With a sinking heart, Thomas explained that he was tracking a rare bird. As he could no longer hear its call he did not ask Germanicus if he was interested in joining the hunt.

Two days. Two failures. But now he had a new plan. A good plan. There was going to be a meteor shower tonight, and the best time to view it was at about three in the morning. He knew that I had a great interest in the beauty of creation, and he spent some time brushing up on the myths and legends that surrounded these cosmic events so that he would be able to eloquently recount them to me while we were lying, star-bound, on the lawn. Several times over the course of the day he phoned our house, but nobody answered.

He figured that was okay. After he had put his aunt to bed, he would come over in person. Only it was not one of her good nights. She was upset, and confused, and had forgotten everything about the last ten years. It wasn't safe to leave her alone.

A little after midnight, he tried ringing one last time. Still no answer. Tired and bitterly disappointed, he went to bed.

But now he couldn't sleep. Outside of his window he could see the first of the shooting stars carving their way across the perfect black of the sky. It had been overcast for much of the day, and now there was his favorite kind of weather: soft drizzle, but mostly clear. The shooting star ducked in behind a cloud, and another emerged where it had disappeared. It was going to be a beautiful show.

LXXVIII

Finally, he got out of bed. He got dressed, put his dog on sentry detail, left the house and walked across the street, standing beneath my window. There were strong vines that ran up the front of the house, and he climbed up them, using the drainpipe to steady himself, until he was standing on the porch roof. Very carefully, he leaned out and tapped on my window. He couldn't quite see inside, but he could tell that the lights were off. Probably I was fast asleep. Courage, he told himself. He had come this far, he only needed to dare a little more. He knocked louder.

There was the sound of a window scraping against its frame, but it was the wrong one. Behind him, someone was opening the window of the spare room. He jumped off the roof and dive-rolled across the lawn, hiding himself in the juniper bushes. First there was the silhouette of the long barrel of a rifle jutting out against the deep grey of the clouds. Then Germanicus' drunken head peered out into the darkness. Thomas became like a rabbit in the bush, perfectly still, waiting. The window closed again and after a few minutes Germanicus came out on the steps, still holding the gun. Thomas doubted that it was loaded, but none the less there was something surreal about being hunted by his best friend.

"Alright. The game's up." Germanicus pointed the rifle dead ahead, at a non-existent target that seemed to be swaying in sloppy circles through the air.

Thomas considered putting his hands up and coming out. But no. There was no way to explain what he was doing in the juniper bush at 2 am.

"Okay, fine. Then, how about a story." Germanicus cocked the gun. "This one's about a guy named Acteon who likes to spy on nymphs. Which is forbidden, because – no, wait. It wasn't nymphs, it was Diana. I don't know why I'm thinking about nymphs..."

Thomas decided that if Germanicus was sufficiently soused to be rolling critical failures on a Greek Mythology check, it was time to flee. Slowly, keeping his belly to the ground, he crawled backwards through the shadows.

"Orpheus! He's the one that the nymphs dismembered. But I mean, really it's all the same: men being torn limb from limb by women. That's the take-home point."

Later, much later, in safety, maybe Thomas would remind his friend that actually Acteon was ripped apart by his own hounds. For now, he needed cover.

He didn't get to it in time.

It was difficult to say whether the shot had been deliberate. There was a moment of stark silence. It felt as if the world were now unreal, and several seconds passed before Thomas could be entirely sure the bullet had missed him. Germanicus was less lucky. He stumbled back, his head cracking against the door-lamp which he mistook for a foe. After several rounds of hand-to-hand combat with the house – a clear win for the lamp-post – Germanicus rolled ass-over-tits over the railing and into the garden below. He made the sound of an injured Muppet.

Thomas stood and dusted himself off. "Is everything okay?" he called out, strolling towards his friend.

"Thomas?" Germanicus was confused. Good. Thomas had been counting on that. "Where did you come from?"

"I was out to watch the stars. I heard a gun. Are you alright?"

"There was a troglodyte...I thought...trying to get into Octavia's bed..."

"Mmm." Thomas dragged Germanicus to his feet and helped him stumble into the house and up the stairs. On a whim, he took a stuffed owl from the altar in the corner of his friend's room and placed it, looking down, right above Germanicus' bed. It was Germanicus' spirit animal, a symbol of wisdom. Thomas got a kick out of the idea that it would reprove him for his behaviour when he woke.

Then, seeing that Germanicus was snoring, he made one last attempt. Softly, softly, he knocked at my bedroom door. I didn't answer, because I wasn't there.

When he got home, he lay down on his front lawn. Overhead, the meteors were streaking across the sky, laying down a tenuous web of light across the darkness. He did his best to delight in their beauty, rather than being disappointed that he had to enjoy it alone.

THE COPPER

SANCTUARY

I must have been delirious. I was lying on my back, I could feel the ground beneath me, the soft mud and the hard rock under it. I could feel the pockets and the hidden boulders. I felt all the sleeping secrets of the earth. I felt that they were my secrets, and its hollows my hollows. Inside of my ribs was a nest of snakes, in the socket of my hip, an ancient skull.

"William?" I spoke to the darkness.

No one answered. I tried to get to my feet. It was strangely easy as if I were light as air. The bottom of the Well had expanded outwards and I realized that I was only sitting in a pool at the bottom of a cavern. From overhead there was a constant dripping of water from strange, opalescent stalagmites. I could see a crevice that might have been the Well shaft and a pale glare. It looked like maybe moonlight that had filtered down a long way, the way that light looks in the deep ocean. Farther in the distance, there were lamps lit in the darkness, curling licks of flame and smudges of grey smoke.

I made my way slowly towards them. The floor was damp and my feet were bare. They barely made a sound as they padded across the wet stone.

I reached the lights. They were copper basins suspended from the rock overhead and filled with burning oil. They cast a glow over the surrounding walls. Copper wire had been wrapped around the stalagmites that rose from the floor, masses of it woven together like bright cocoons. As it rose the copper was shaped into trees and pillars, walls and thrones. There was no scheme to it, it was more like a gallery than a landscape. Woven into the copper there were countless thousands of stones and shards of stone. I pried one of them out and held it up to the light. It had once been part of a large, flat river-rock but it had been deliberately shattered. Looking around to see that no one was watching me I placed the shard like a lozenge on my tongue.

In an instant I was transported away from the cavern and into a fragment of another world. A large hall with a table in the middle of it. A feast of some sort had been laid out: figs and dates, olives and fermented fish. A suggestion of sea-breeze seemed to come from some distant window but it was hard to make it out. The world seemed to have been disrupted, incompleted. People hovered in the shadows at the edge of my vision but I couldn't get them to come into focus. Every so often there was a little piece of language, a touch of laughter, a gaze that could clearly be seen, and then nothing again. Whatever narrative had been commended to this stone had lost its coherence when the stone was broken.

I removed it from my mouth and put it back in its place. Very slowly I made my way among the copper statuary. It seemed to go on almost endlessly, winding back into the darkness with the walls closing in to either side. At the end of the cavern there was a pool and a copper tree reaching its roots down into the water. Hanging from the boughs were human bones. I reached up and plucked one of them. It was hung with a short piece of wire and came away easily. The bone of a child. William's bones. I was sure of it. With tears forming at the corners of my eyes I began to gather them all up. Tiny hand bones, and long slender radii, Thick square bones of the sort that used to be thrown for dice. Finally a skull. I gathered them into my backpack so that I would be able to bear them out of here and give them a proper burial.

When they were plucked I started to make my way back to where I had begun. I felt as if I could hear someone following me but whenever I stopped the footfalls stopped as well. I tried to tell myself that it couldn't be an echo because the slapping sound wasn't quite the same as the one that my own feet made.

"Hello?"

There was a softly indrawn breath. I couldn't tell if the person in the darkness was trying to keep silent because they were stalking me or because they were afraid.

"Hello?" I tried to sound unthreatening and not scared.

A figure darted towards me and grabbed me by the hand. It was William, small, and gaunt but otherwise exactly as he had been when he was lost to the Well. "You have to get out of here Vivi." He tugged on me urgently, "You have to get out of here." He was pulling me so hard that I nearly stumbled to the ground. "Do you understand what you've done?"

I shook my head. "No. What do you mean?"

"Don't you remember the story?" He stopped pulling and he looked at me very urgently.

"What story?"

He looked impatient. "When Hades took Persephone down into the darkness, that wasn't the end of the story. Don't you remember what happened next?"

"She --" I stopped, understanding. "She ate a single pomegranate seed. That's why she couldn't go back."

THE MIND KILLER

I held William's hand, and we ran as if we could outpace fate. When we arrived at the pool he ordered me to crouch down and cover my face. At first, I peered out through my fingers to see what he was doing but then I remembered that this was how Orpheus had lost his opportunity to lead Eurydice out of the underworld; this was how Psyche had lost her Cupid. If you were told to cover your eyes, then you could not, no matter what happened, look.

Frightened, I huddle in the darkness until my haunches were so numb that I started to fall over. I put my hand out. It met stone. "William?" I whispered, but there was only silence. I opened my eyes. The walls of reality had closed back in and I realized that I was still curled up at the bottom of the Well. I blinked and stretched, and a sharp stabbing pain reminded me that my leg was still hurt. Perhaps hurt even worse than it had been before.

I told myself I must have been dreaming, because no way had I been able to run. Not with my leg like this. I looked up and realized that the moon had almost moved out of view. You could see only a fingernail sliver of light curling along the black edge of the Well. I was trapped, and soon it was going to be completely dark. A sob shook my ribs as I realized how impossible my position was.

"There is no such thing as a hopeless situation."

For sure I was hallucinating again. A bead of orange-red hovered in the darkness. It moved towards the sillhouette of a man. There was a slow, sucking, indrawn breath and the bead lengthened, brightened. It was the tip of a cigarette, and it was being smoked by my brother. I knew it was a vision because Germanicus so doesn't smoke. "I'm trapped," I protested. "And I'm scared."

"Fear is the mind killer," Germanicus said evenly. "You can get out of here. You just have to try."

"Try how?"

"What do you see if you look up?"

"Nothing really. The night sky. A couple of stars."

"If you can see light, then you can climb. I would do it like this," he pulled his knees up towards himself and jammed his feet against the wall of the Well so that the small of his back was pressed hard into the stone. "Then I would very slowly inch my way up."

"And what if you fell?"

"Then I would start over again."

"Easy for you to say. Look at my leg," I gestured, showing him how it was swollen and useless.

"You think that hurts? Try long starvation. Trust me, it gets worse."

I started to cry again. He looked away as if he were ashamed of my fear. "Look," I said, pulling myself together. "It's not like I want to die. It's just that...There's no point." I explained the thing about Persephone and the pomegranate seed.

"Don't be stupid." Germanicus finished his cigarette and crushed the stub against the side of the Well. A few embers fell and extinguished themselves on the surface of the water. "You have muscles, you have willpower, and you can see the way out. Your fate isn't determined by a fairy tale."

"What if it is?" I whispered hopelessly. Germanicus didn't answer, and now, without the cigarette, I couldn't even see him in the dark. I reached out, but there was nobody there.

Somehow, now that I could no longer argue with him, I felt the need to spite him by proving that I could do it without his coaching. I could be as strong in real life as he was in his fantasies, and I could be resourceful too. I opened my backpack.

It was full of the bones that I had gathered from the tree: their musty smell, their smooth surfaces. They were so realistic. Did that mean that they were real? I put the question out of my mind as I rifled through them, searching for the length of rope lurking in the bottom of the bag. I took it out and wound it around the largest of the bones. I tossed it up as high as I could, hoping that it would go out over the the edge of the Well and find something to catch on. It didn't go even half-way up the well shaft, and then it fell down again, hitting me in the shoulder. I winced.

Clearly, I wasn't going to get out that way. I decided that I would climb like Germanicus said. I wedged myself in, my shoulders on one side of the well shaft and my good leg on the other with my bad one sort of crooked sideways resting on my knee. I could get up a couple of feet, but no further. With only one leg there was no way that I was going to be able to climb up.

Another dead end. I was starting to feel frantic. Maybe I could call on Jupiter to come and fish me out. Or ask the spirit of the spring to carry me up. If only I had been a real Roman girl I might have placed my hope in such things.

The only thing was, I was going to have to climb the ordinary way. I was going to have make use of both of my legs, and both of my hands, and it wasn't going to matter at all how much it hurt. That was that. There was no other way.

I began to climb. I could feel my mind sort of separating itself from my body in between foot and handholds. Every time that I put weight on my left foot, it pulled my consciousness back in and I could feel again. It made me sick and I realized that I was making a hideous sound, like in between a war cry and a child's wailing.

Time does not behave normally under conditions like that. It opened and closed like a mouth, now swallowing me, now spitting me out on the shores of awareness. I realized that I had slipped and fallen, but I just got up and started again, mechanically, uncaring. I don't know how many times that happened. Just that eventually I was there, where the ground had given way, at the top of the Well.

I lay on a cushion of dew-damp leaves, the stars spinning dizzily above my head. Whisps of breath, white in the cold night air, drifted up from my lips. I wondered if they would send search teams out to find me, on a path that wasn't there, and imagined that maybe one day I would hobble out of the woods to find that a hundred years had passed while I slept in a faerie grove. I closed my eyes.

☺   ☺   ☺

William stands at the bottom of the well, looking up. It's the first time since he walked across the bridge and into Antonio's kingdom that he has been allowed to come out here where you can see up out of the top of the Well. He shudders in spite of himself. He's grown used to his home, but not to this horrid place with its oily waters and its carpet of rough, unprocessed stones whispering their evils into the silent air. "She will come back, right?" Even though he whispers, his voice reverberates and he can hear his own anxiety amplified by water and stone.

"Be patient," Antonio's hand falls on his shoulder.

"I just don't see why she couldn't have stayed. She was right here. I could have asked her."

"And she would have said 'No.' You must be patient and wait until she is ready to say 'Yes' of her own accord."

William kicks at the stones. His toe catches on something hard. "Her backpack!" His panic echoes in the darkness, and Antonio places a finger hard against his lips. "She forgot it!"

"My child, how could she have carried it herself? Jules will take it up to her while she sleeps."

William considers this and sees that his fear was ill-placed. "Couldn't I take it?"

Antonio smiles patiently. A length of silken cord slithers into his hand from nowhere. With a flourish, he throws it into the air. It shoots upwards and then just hangs there as if pinned to the sky. "Very well then. Here you are."

The moment that William's fingers close on the rope, a deep tremor passes through him. Determined, he grips it tight, wrapping it around his palms and attempts to climb. Weariness consumes him. He can hear all of his bones crackling like cellophane and his skin feels paper dry. He lets go and collapses, breathing heavily, kneeling on one knee in the water. When he has recovered his breath, Antonio takes him by the elbow and lifts him to his feet. "Come on home," he says. "You got to see her tonight. And she'll be with you soon enough."

ACT II

ELEMENTARY

The thick opalescent fog that hung over London nearly obscured the view which the window at 221B Baker Street afforded of the street below. I therefore caught only the slightest glimpse of the figure that ran down the street, weaving past the early morning workmen and the hansom cabs on their way to appointments in the city. The door below opened, and there came a tumultuous rush of feet in the hall and on the stair. A moment later a pale, dishevelled and wide-eyed young man, visibly palpitating, burst into the room.

"Octavia is missing." This strange reconnaisance he delivered in a tone of strictly reined panic, as though he had every confidence that my friend, Sherlock Holmes, would both comprehend the matter and consent to aid in its happy resolution.

Holmes looked up from where he was bent over the microscope, intently investigating a piece of counterfiet coinage. "Pray compose yourself," he instructed. "You may provide me with an account of your little difficulty when you are calm."

The youth suppressed a look of profound irritation. He settled himself on the carpet and folded his legs in that curious manner which I believe is popular among the mystics of the East. A most remarkable change passed swiftly over his features. I could scare believe how quickly I found myself gazing into an alert, intelligent and rather comely face whose impassivity almost equalled that of Holmes himself. "The facts are as follows."

He leapt to his feet and crossed to a blackboard which hung on Holmes' wall. Unceremoniously rubbing some chemical calculations from its face, he wrote a date and a time: *Sunday, 12:55pm – Mary and Jerome Kirkman leave for Australia. 1:00pm – Send Octavia to practice Lyre. Rescue canoe from pond,* etc.

Never had I seen a client relate his story in such minute and perfect detail, nor encountered one capable of drawing deductions before my friend had a chance to observe them himself. It was this fact, more than any other, that first made me suspect the identity of our curious visitor.

Some years earlier, Holmes and I had been induced to abandon 19th Century London and to remove ourselves to the Interior Fortress of a young man by the name of Germanicus Kirkman. This Fortress was a fantastical locale roughly based on the Jesuitical art of constructing a Memory Palace: that is, a reproduction in the mind of some physical location where mnemonic information may be stored in visual form. Holmes had been attracted by the interesting additions which young Kirkman had made to the discipline, and so he had consented to join the select circle of geniuses that our host had assembled to help him unravel particularly troubling problems in his private life.

Thus it was that we had been comfortably installed in the environs of Mr. Kirkman's imagination. He was, by all accounts, an intelligent, moderate and sobre youth. I was therefore surprised to note a lingering scent of anise-infused spirits and the distinctive symptoms of a hangover.

"So, that brings us up to the events of this morning." My attention had drifted somewhat from the curt recitation of minutiae which had formed the backbone of our client's story. "When I finally got around to listening to the answering machine message from Octavia's school." He spoke with a singular accent that bore, I thought, some distant resemblance to the American. Strange coinages like "face book" peppered his discourse, which was at times so ungrammatical as to scarcely permit comprehension. Holmes, however, seemed to have no difficulty interpreting these eccentricities.

Holmes held up his hand, "There is some matter that you have ommitted. I observe that you give a very complete account of events up until noon yesterday, and then you completely pass over a period of more than ten hours."

Mr. Kirkman looked away in obvious embarrasment. "That isn't relevant. Octavia was gone well before I got home."

"Indeed. By my calculation it is some 36 hours since you last laid eyes on your sister."

"Yes." His shame was palpable.

"Go on."

"Well, I kind of assume that there's a boy involved. Mom has always been a little...overprotective, and I can't think of an innocent reason why someone would have been knocking at her window in the middle of the night."

"Yes. Obviously, some young Lethario decided to abduct your sister at seven o'clock yesterday morning, and then returned to seduce her nearly a full twenty hours after he had already achieved his designs. A most promising line of reasoning, don't you agree Watson?"

The boy blinked several times and I could see that he was looking upon his recent troubles in an entirely different light. "Stupid," he said. "Yes, you're right, of course. But then where is she? And what the blazes is she doing?"

"That," said Holmes dryly, "is precisely the matter at hand. But there is, I think, some queer feature of his case that has compelled you to bring it to my attention, is there not?"

C

"Right. The owl."

Holmes, for the first time, had that hungry look which indicates that a case might hold some interest for his penetrating intellect. "Pray, continue."

"Probably it's best if I just show you."

The owl in question was perched atop the headboard of an ascetically furnished captain's bed. It was an impressive specimen, of North American extraction, preserved with both of its wings outstretched and mounted on a circle of brightly polished wood. "It was here, staring me down when I woke up this morning. It definitely wasn't there last night."

"Intriguing," Holmes lifted the animal from its resting place and subjected it to a minute examination.

"It usually sits over there," our client pointed towards a small shelf on the far side of the room where there stood a votive statuette of Athene, about twelve inches in height, and a small censor, recently used. "Someone moved it in the night."

Holmes' attention was fixed on the headboard. "When was this shelf last dusted?"

"Saturday. Mom insisted that everything be spotless before she left."

"In that case, we may conclude that this," he ran his finger through a faint line of chalky dust that ran along the mahogany coloured wood, "came to be here within the last

48 hours. If I am not mistaken, it is something akin to plaster..."

Kirkman joined Holmes in examining the fine white powder. "Drywall dust."

At the same moment, both men looked up at the ceiling. There was hatch there, presumably leading to the attic. In a second, our client had climbed up and removed it. With considerable alacrity he pulled himself up into the narrow aperture. I noted, with some small satisfaction in my own powers of observation, that his exertions had left behind a small scattering of dust identical to that found beneath the owl.

After a moment his head reappeared. "One of Octavia's year-boxes is missing. From when she was ten."

"Did anything of note occur during that year?"

"To be honest, it's a bit blurry. I had jaw surgery. Twice. And they botched it both times. I spent most of the year doped up on prescription opiates. However..." I could see that he was trying to reconstruct a memory out of broken fragments. His contemplations culminated in the ejaculation of a thoroughly unprintable expression. "That's the year William went missing."

"An acquiantance of your sister's?"

"I really hope this has nothing to do with him."

"Can you think of any reason why your sister might have taken a renewed interest in this missing boy?"

Our client's eyes closed and he looked as though he was organizing some invisible catalogue in his mind. "Blast! Yes. Sunday was the anniversary of William's death."

"Well, in that case let's see if we can't find the missing box."

The girl's room was clean, neatly organized, though one had the impression that this was a recent innovation. A delicate floral pattern in shades of lilac and blue decorated the walls and a dressmaker's dummy stood in the corner wearing a flowing skirt, pinned together and marked with tailor's chalk. The bed was neatly made and a linen night-dress tucked under the pillow.

Holmes opened the window and set a cigarette alight. "Ah. This is where our intruder came knocking last night. Now what did he see, and why did it cause him to break into your room and shuffle the taxidermy about? This case does have some interesting features."

Holmes clambered out onto the roof and stood looking into the room. "He knocks on your sister's window, and sees that she is not asleep inside --"

"It was bright last night. Gibbous moon. Definitely light enough to make it difficult to see into a darkened room."

"Possibly. Unless the moonlight were coming in through the side window, in which case the porch would have been in shadow. Let's see...last night, at four o'clock, the moon should have been --" I could see the celestial spheres revolving in that wonderful machine that is Holmes' mind.

"Over there," the boy got to the answer first. "You're right. It's possible you would have been able to see into the room, but the bed would still have been in shadow."

"It may be... No. I feel certain we're missing something." Holmes edged towards the drainpipe, looking down. "Now, that is significant."

"What?"

"Look at the ground. You can see where your intruder has leapt from the roof. Yet there is also a patch of flattened foliage in the garden, much closer to the house, which is certaintly suggestive..."

A deep groan escaped our client's lips. "You don't need to investigate that. I completely forgot... certain... details... of last night."

Some dark combination of disappointment and irriration momentarily troubled Holmes' countenance. "Spit it out, man."

"I kind of made an idiot of myself. The sordid minutiae are not important. At least I know who's responsible for the owl. Thomas must have put it there when he put me to bed...his idea of a joke."

Holmes looked at once quizzical and bored. Young Kirkman sank into silent self-recrimination. Seeing that further details were not forthcoming, Holmes' attention turned in another direction. "Hi ho!" he cried. "What have we here?" He practically leapt back in through the window, his eyes fixed upon the skirt of the bed. "This room, like yours, was tidied recently, yet here we see a box stuffed in under the bed at an angle of some 36 degrees."

Our client shuddered, as though such derilection from a purely orthoganol arrangement caused him pain. The box was produced. Germanicus opened the lid and spread its contents over the bed. "I don't see anything that has to do with William here. But..." He had picked up a stack of small paper squares which were completely blank. An old piece of bright-pink ribbon was tucked in around them. "These belonged to Cataline. She left them out on the island. Only..." he looked deeply perturbed. "They had writing on them."

"It is possible," suggested Holmes, "that only the top sheet contained an inscription, and that the rest were left blank so as to suggest a long missive when in fact there was only a brief note. I have seen it done."

"It might have been possible," the youth replied, "except that this is clearly the top page." He lifted one piece of the rough, cream-coloured stationary and displayed it to Holmes. "You see?"

"Yes. It has been left in the damp, and the dye from the ribbon has left a clear discolouration on the surface of the page. But then, my dear Kirkman, you must admit that it was not written upon. For there no sign of ink, nor even that residual indendation that would remain if the note were written in some impermanent fluid."

"I admit to an inability to explain the facts. I do not admit to a fault in my memory. There was writing on those pages when she put them down." I could see something in his eyes akin to fear, and I sensed that he was contemplating some supernatural solution abhorrent to my friend.

"Let us leave that for now. I think we have enough evidence to say with confidence that your sister went missing sometime yesterday, that she entered your room after you left for school –"

"Yeah. I don't know how she got in. The doors were locked..."

"By using the dumb-waiter. I thought that was obvious." Holmes was smoking quite rapidly now. "She left the house no earlier than eight o'clock, and her absence most likely relates to the loss of her childhood friend." The cigarette had burned itself down to his fingers. "I can only advise you summon the police."

"Yeah, Sherlock, listen. I know you get on with the cops because you solve all of their cases for them. My family, on the other hand, offers bloody sacrifice to gods that nobody has worshipped in over a thousand years, and my sister was at the centre of the disappearance of a child who was never found. I'm only contacting the authorities if I have literally no other choice."

Holmes raised his eyebrows. "In that case, you had better hope that the ground was soft and that your sister hasn't gone far. I, after all, am nothing more than a figment of your imagination and I don't believe that tracking is among your skills."

That agitation which had marked the young man' features upon our first meeting began to return and he wrung one of his hands as he began to pace the room.

"If I might make a suggestion," I interjected. Both men turned to look at me, "It seems that your friend, the one who put you to bed, what did you say his name was?"

"Thomas."

"Well," I cleared my throat, determined to be discreet, "under the circumstances his memory of the events might be clearer than your own."

"Of course!" he stopped, smacking himself dead in the centre of his brow. "Thomas!" Already he was running out of the room, down the stairs and onto the porch.

There, on the concrete step, was the clear shape of an arrow outlined in small stones. It pointed towards a pasture where goats were gamboling on the backs of low green hills. Germanicus paused a moment, the tension in his shoulders subsiding however slightly, "And apparently he's way ahead of me." He smiled at me and at Holmes. "You can go back to Baker Street now. From here on, I suspect it will all be quite elementary."

IN THE SKIN
OF A SNAKE

The forest was dark. I was under the shadow of a massive tree, an ancient pine whose branches went up like a ladder into the cloud-shrouded sky. I was hanging up the bones, like Christmas ornaments, but in the shape of a body. Filaments snaked down from the boughs twining around the bones and binding them into place. A small army of spiders started to ascend from the earth, eight-legged jewels with strange sigils painted on their tiny backs. They climbed my body like a mountain. My belly had been torn open and there was something inside of it, shining and terrible, a stone or a pit. The spiders poured around it as they climbed towards the skeleton. They sewed the bones together encasing them in a flesh of silk. William's face, slowly, slowly was beginning to take shape. His mouth opened. I reached inside and felt the teeth clamp down on my fingers. There was something hidden inside. I could reach it, but my fingers had been severed and I could not grasp.

☺　　☺　　☺

Thomas crouched low to the ground, his head cocked to one side, studying the soil. At first, tracking me was simple. My boots had a short heel and it had left a deep imprint, easy to see even in the murky grey dawnlight. Sometimes there were objects dropped or discarded, like the little green whistle that nestled in the brush at the bottom of a small cliff. Thomas picked it up and blew into it. It made a sound like an injured loon. He scrambled up the rock face until he found a small patch of moss had been broken like a torn membrane, revealing a sinkhole. There was a little blood, not much, but it suggested that once upon a time my ankle had been in that hole and that I had suffered in getting it free.

Now, he was at the top of the rock-face. He could see the imprint the folds in my skirt had left on the soil. Then a trail, not walking but crawling, one leg dragging along behind. And then a mystery. The trail ended abruptly at a patch of a wild blackberries. There was no evidence of the growth having been disturbed.

Thomas sat and considered the situation. Nearby, there was a small patch of grass-like greenery. He picked some of it, made a small fire, and threw the grass on top of it as an offering to the spirits that lived in this part of the forest. For a long time the herb smouldered with a sweet-smelling hiss, and then there was a sympathetic rustle from the clump from which he had picked it. A small, beautiful bronze snake was making its way through the underbrush. Thomas sank down onto his belly and became the snake, slithering softly in underneath the thorns.

After a long time he stood up. Behind him, the bushes had closed back on the path so that he could see no evidence of his own passage. The first of the early morning sunlight was just starting to trickle in askance through the dense undergrowth. Ahead, a strange path wound among unfamiliar trees.

☉   ☉   ☉

The teeth of the forest floor were biting deep into my back but I couldn't make myself roll over. I could hear voices in the distance calling my name, like Echo calling for Narcissus. I listened to them bouncing off of the trees and almost felt like I could see the sound, geometric arcs tracing themselves web-like through the forest. The voices were strangely familiar, child-like, singing to me from the depths of the Well. I laid back and sang to them silently, and each time they answered, louder, rising, falling, passing like ghosts or ships in the night.

The ground heaved suddenly beneath me and I was lifted up. Disoriented, I realized that it wasn't the ground at all but the sky that was wrapping me up in swaddling cloths of cold air. The voices fractured and transformed into birdsong.

My fingers, like Prometheus's liver, had grown back. I twisted them into the collar of a familiar sweater. There was a scent of tobacco, but not of smoke. Overhead, the clouds were swirling in sickening circles and a harpy-scream broke the chill morning air. "Shhh, shhh. I know it hurts," a soft voice said. That was when I realized that the screams were coming from myself.

☺   ☺   ☺

When I woke up there was a campfire burning next to me and an emergency blanket swaddled my legs. I smelled roasting meat and heard the juices bubbling down into the flames. I tried to push myself up and was immediately answered by a swift, fiery ache sweeping through my body. I cried out and sank back down onto the cold earth.

Thomas was suddenly beside me, offering me a small, collapsible tin cup full of water. I was so thirsty I didn't even ask how he had gotten there. As I drank, he picked up a stick off the fire and turned it over. I realized that the meat which had smelled so appetizing a moment ago was a large, blackened snake, its skin blistered and bursting like a malignant sausage.

"The snake is looking after you today," he said pleasantly. Noticing how I wrinkled my nose he added, "It doesn't taste that bad."

"It's okay," I said weakly. "I'll eat when we get home." I looked around, but I couldn't move my neck very far. Apart from the fire I could see a massive pile of leaves that Thomas had clearly been gathering together, and a wooden frame that looked alarmingly as though it planned to develop into a shelter.

"Your leg is broken. You're not ready to move."

"Then shouldn't you be calling for help?" I imagined a helicopter sweeping down into the clearing, its blades skimming against the bent boughs of the trees.

"It's very easy to get lost in this forest," he said, not really answering me. "The ground is unsettled here. A long time ago, the glaciers carried things down here from the North, things that never belonged in this place. The bones of mammoths, maybe. Usually that isn't a problem, because the dust comes, and the rain, and everything gets covered up. Hills form above all the secret things that the earth is hoarding. They're given a proper burial and laid to rest. But every so often you find a place where the ground isn't settled, and then it can be very dangerous and very easy to get lost."

"You know this forest," I reminded him. "You won't get lost."

"I don't think it would be safe to leave you." He picked up the roast snake from on top of the fire and began peeling away its skin with his pocket knife. "Here," he speared a bite and offered it to me. When at first I didn't take it, he simply sat there, holding it about three inches from my face while he continued to stir the fire.

"Can't you build a stretcher then?"

"Sure. A stretcher. One that will allow me to carry you single-handed down 3 metres of sheer basalt. I will make it out of pine needles and fresh bamboo. No, better. How about I make a cell-phone out of a coconut." He wiggled the knife slightly.

I took a deep breath and relented. I picked the greasy piece of flesh off the end of his knife. It tasted bad, and not at all like chicken, but at least it didn't make me feel sick.

When I'd eaten as much as I could, I curled my arm miserably under my head and looked into the curling tongues of Thomas' campfire. I desperately wanted to be curled up in my bed with a hot cup of tea, but instead I was stuck out here in the woods, with a hard, knotted root digging itself into my hip. I tried to shift to get more comfortable, but there was another lick of pain and I started shivering so hard that my teeth chattered uncontrollably. Thomas came over and stretched his body on the ground next to mine, pressing himself very gently against me so that he didn't disturb any of my limbs. His arm curled around my stomach, warm and weightless. "I don't have any more blankets," he apologized. "And you need to stay warm."

The shivering slowly subsided. I twined my fingers around his and held on tight. It suddenly hit me, how grateful I ought to be that I hadn't woken up alone out here with no one to take care of me. I mumbled, belatedly, "Thank you for the snake."

MALUM

"Explanation. Complete. Unabridged. Now."
Germanicus glowered down at me, like a thunderbolt
clasped in the hand of Zeus. I blinked, trying to clear the
sleep from my eyes, and mumbled something incoherent.
He knelt, grabbed my shoulders and shook me awake. I
screamed as the pain ricocheted down into my leg. He let go.
He didn't apologize. "Why did you take off?"

I began trying to explain, cautiously at first, leaving
a lot of things out. My brother wasn't having it. He
questioned every omission, called me on inconsistencies,
demanded more detail whenever I was vague.

As Germanicus interrogated me, Thomas knelt by the fire, measuring out herbs that he had brought with him in a small leather bag. I was exhausted, trembling from the effort of trying to satisfy my brother's thirst for information, when Thomas handed me a cup of tea. It tasted like bitter roots and pungent earth with overtones of mint, and it made me feel relaxed and slightly giddy. I nestled my head into the pillow of leaves that Thomas had made for me, and listened to the breeze rustling overhead. Germanicus asked me yet another question, but I just giggled softly. "I don't remember, Germanicus. I don't remember anything else," I murmured, closing my eyes.

Germanicus decided to let it go for now. He got up and walked to the other side of the campsite, speaking quietly to Thomas, "She seems pretty delirious, but... I don't really see why a broken leg would cause hallucinations."

"She isn't delirious. Delirious people talk about transcendental giraffes, and where they put their rutabaga. They don't tell coherent stories, and they can't be questioned about the details. Either she's telling you what really happened, or she's deliberately lying. The question is, do you trust her or not?"

"Thomas, seriously. We're not in a novel by C. S. bloody Lewis. In the real world, if somebody claims to have met a faun in the furniture they're either concussed or dropping acid."

Thomas paused. "Come here. I think there's something you should see."

I heard a slight rattle as he placed something on the ground, and then the sound of a wet zipper being slowly teased open. "*Malum,*" said Germanicus, removing a human skull from my backpack.

Thomas squatted beside him. "Six years ago, William's bones were not in these woods. I do not believe they were even in this world."

"Hold on..." Germanicus put the skull down and started removing the other bones from the backpack. He laid them out on the ground, saying their names to himself as he built them, jigsaw-like, into the skeleton of a child. He swore again in Latin, this time more under his breath. It wasn't a word I recognized.

"It's okay," I mumbled. The shadows in the pine trees behind Germanicus were really pretty, a moving tapestry of different greens. "I've found him now. Now I know he's dead," a lump formed in my throat. Until I'd said it, I hadn't quite realized what finding his skeleton meant.

"Right. Sure. Except these bones are not William O'Hare's."

I blinked, trying to focus. Thomas looked perplexed. "They must be."

"No. William was ten when he died, this child was five, maybe six. Look," he pointed at something I couldn't see. "As the bone structure develops there are cartilaginous tissues that ossify during childhood, so the number of bones changes with age. Also, look at the teeth," he lifted the skull and pointed towards the molars, then, very suddenly, cut short his lecture and stared at the jaw in confusion. "Weird."

"What?"

"Well, I would have thought that the connective tissues between the mandible and the maxilla would have liquified as the body decayed. But he's still got his jaw clamped tight."

"Let me see," with difficulty, I extended my hand. Germanicus handed me the skull. Now that I was looking at it clearly, I could see that it wasn't William's. The cheekbones were all wrong, and the jaw was too square. For a moment I could almost see the face that had once filled out these empty bones: two blue eyes looking up at me from out of the sockets, glazed and uncomprehending as they stared out into some nameless sorrow. "You're right," I said, returning the skull. "It isn't him."

"Hold on, there's something in there." Germanicus was rattling the skull gently, holding it up as if he expected it to whisper a secret in his ear. "Thomas, can I borrow your knife?"

"If you think it wise." He removed a hunting knife from his belt and handed it to my brother. Germanicus pushed the point in between the teeth of the strange child and pried open its jaw. Bone cracked and splintered. He reached his fingers in and for a moment I thought that the spirit of the boy would come back and would clamp its teeth down on my brother's knuckles, but that didn't happen. Instead, Germanicus fished something out of the hollow of

CXVIII

its broken jaw. A stone. Perfectly smooth, white-grey, criss-crossed with delicate fault lines. It looked as if the child had rolled it around in his mouth for a long time, sucking on it like a lozenge until every imperfection had been worn away.

"Give it here," I said, reaching towards it hungrily. Germanicus handed it to me, and I was about to put it to my lips when he snatched it back.

"What are you doing?" he demanded. "That's been inside the mouth of a dead person for... I don't even know how long." He shot a worried look at Thomas.

Thomas took the stone from Germanicus, studied it for a moment and put it in his pocket. "The tea I gave her contained some potent pain-killers. She may not be so lucid."

Germanicus sat for a moment, studying the skeleton. "We've got to bury these," he said at last.

"This is a missing child. We have to turn this in to the police."

Germanicus shook his head. "Thomas, you remember when William disappeared. For like a month we had the entire apparatus of the nanny-state camped out in our living room, asking stupid questions every time anyone breathed. There's no way I'm putting my parents through that again."

"What about the parents of this child?"

"You're the one who says you believe Octavia's story. If you honestly think there's a supernatural evil in this forest, what good are cops gonna be?"

The two boys stared each other down for a couple of minutes. Thomas finally looked away. "We can talk about this later," he said. "I'll find somewhere to hide the bones for now."

"Fine." Germanicus picked up the backpack and started shredding it into long strips with Thomas' knife. "We need to get Octavia out of here as quickly as possible. I'll build a stretcher. You see if you can throw together a half-decent splint."

Thomas borrowed my brother's sweater and used it to carefully bundle up the bones. He disappeared for a while. When he came back, he had some long straight branches that he used to bind up my broken leg. It hurt, but I bit my lip hard and managed not to cry. Germanicus, in the meantime, used the canvas strips from the backpack to build the world's most uncomfortable litter out of sticks. They settled me on it, and then spent a while bickering about which of several different kinds of semi-impassable terrain would be easier to navigate. Eventually they settled on a route and picked me up.

The stretcher groaned and sagged. "I don't think this is stable," said Thomas.

"Yeah, well we don't have anything better. She'll just have to hold on tight."

My knuckles curled white around the rails. Every step jostled my leg as we pitched over the rocky slopes. "Stop," I cried after forever. "Please. Just put me down."

CXX

A sharp jolt. Several of the sticks cracked as Thomas came to a halt. "Keep going!" Germanicus ordered from behind.

"She needs to rest."

"It's been less than five minutes. We've got at least an hour to go."

I started to cry. It hurt so much.

"She's not going to make it."

"She'll be fine. It's just pain."

"I'm going to put her down."

Thomas began to crouch. Germanicus didn't follow suit. I lay staring up through the canopy, gulping back sobs. Finally my brother relented and I was lowered to the ground.

"I'm not being cruel," he said. "That tea you made her is already starting to wear off. The longer we drag our asses, the worse it's gonna get."

"I don't want to go home anymore," I whimpered. "I like it here. I'll be good. I'll eat up all my snake."

Thomas laid a hand on my shoulder, apologized and resumed his post.

Germanicus snapped a stick off a nearby bush. With the bedside manner of a Legionary, he stuck it between my teeth. "Bite down hard. This is the last time we stop."

CXXI

DOCTOR

APPLEWOOD

A hospital room split down the middle by a sickly green shroud. On the other side of the curtain, a strange family was visiting an unknown man. My attention was distracted, fixed on a small boy's feet that kept rocking back and forth near a piece of old spit out gum on the floor. I kept wondering whether he would step on the gum and whether, if he did, the gum would stick to the bottom of his shoes. Sometimes things don't stick. They'd given me a shot of something. Maybe that was why I was so interested in the question of the gum. Or maybe it was because it reminded me of something else.

People kept coming in and out of the room. They asked me questions. Sometimes the questions were innocent, like "You feeling okay?" Sometimes they were dangerous. I had to remember what Germanicus had told me: "You don't have to lie. In fact, I abjure you not to lie. You just have to tell the truth...judiciously." He had outlined a version of the truth for me, one that didn't involve William, or bones, or caverns of copper and stone. I had trouble remembering it, though.

There was one doctor in particular who didn't seem to be satisfied. She had a sharp nose, short hair and blue-green bifocals. Her lips were tight, her skin clung a little too closely to her cheek-bones, and her voice had a measured kindness to it that set me on edge. She was a psychologist named Doctor Applewood, and she kept asking me questions that Germanicus hadn't rehearsed with me: "Why did you go out in the woods alone?" "Is it normal that you would have been out all night?" "Why do you think your brother didn't contact the police?"

"Octavia," her voice was gentle, but insistent. I had been staring at the bubble gum on the bottom of the shoe for too long.

I scratched a little at the thin, clear plastic that kept my IV stuck into my arm. "He tried to call," I lied, "but he couldn't get reception. I didn't want him to leave me alone."

"I thought there were two boys?"

CXXIII

"I don't know," I said, trying not to sound confused. "Maybe you should ask them."

She made a note. Her pencil had recently been sharpened, and there was one crystal of graphite that was harder than the others. It scratched against the pad like a claw. She finished writing and patted my hand. "You've certainly been through a lot," she said, "and you're very brave. It must have been frightening, to be out there all alone at night." She paused, "Did it bring back any memories?"

I shifted uncomfortably. My leg was in some kind of temporary thing to keep it still while they waited for the X-rays, and I couldn't move much. "What kind of memories?"

"Didn't you lose your friend in the woods, when you were a child?"

I swallowed hard. Germanicus hadn't briefed me on this. "How do you know about William?"

"You and I talked, Octavia, after he disappeared. Do you not remember?" I shook my head. "Maybe because I wore contacts then." She removed her glasses. No. I still couldn't remember her at all.

"It was a long time ago," I said.

"Do you think about him much?"

"William," I could hear my voice cracking. "Oh. I don't know. Sometimes." The judiciously edited truth was now coming out in a high-pitched, incriminating squeak.

"It's okay," Doctor Applewood said gently. "That's normal. It must have been very difficult for you to find people to talk to. There was a lot of nasty gossip, I think."

My throat tightened, and a stupid kid's song about being eaten by a boa-constrictor started looping in my head. "People said I lied. Some even said it was my fault."

Her bifocals nodded sympathetically. She opened her mouth to ask another question, but was interrupted by a rustling at the curtain. I breathed a sigh of relief: my brother had arrived. Germanicus came bearing a bouquet of wildflowers stuck in a mason jar. He placed them beside my bed and gave me a quick kiss. "From Thomas," he said. "The flowers, not the kiss."

Doctor Applewood stood back and gave us a moment to exchange pleasantries, then extended her hand towards my brother and introduced herself. "If you don't mind," she said, "I'd like to talk with you a moment. Perhaps outside?" she gestured towards the hall.

Since Germanicus' expressions are almost completely indistinguishable to the casual observer, probably she didn't notice how anxious he was. "Sure," he said. "No prob."

They put a cast on my leg, and I floated home on a cushion of painkillers. My brother carried me in and settled me on the old sofa in my father's study. He built up a fire, tucked the blankets in around me and brought me a cup of sleepy tea. I sipped it slowly, savouring the soft minty aroma

CXXV

while Germanicus sat nearby fiddling around on a tablet. I dozed off.

I was jolted awake by the sound of a fist striking wood. Feeling that there must be some danger, I sat up too fast. "What is it?"

My brother's palm was pressed hard against the wooden arm of the chair. "We're in trouble," he said.

"How do you mean?"

"You know that headshrinker that gave me the third degree about why I didn't call the cops? Look," he showed me the screen.

"Those are William's school records! How did you get that?"

"The internet," he said, as though this was a more-than-sufficient explanation. "Here," he pointed, "you see that? The school counselor referred William to a psychologist a couple of weeks before he died." I wanted to correct him about William being dead, but he moved on too fast. "And if you look at his medical records," he tabbed over to another document that he should not have been able to access, "you can see that the psychologist in question is a Doctor Patricia Applewood. Unfortunately, she's either smart enough, or old-school enough, not to keep her records on a system that anyone can just hack into. So we don't know what William told her – or, for that matter, exactly what you said to her all those years ago."

"Calm down, Germanicus," I took a sip of my tea and tried to clear my system of the second-hand anxiety that my brother was breathing into the room. "So this Applewood woman is maybe suspicious. So what?"

"So, she practically ordered me to bring you to her office later this week."

I shrugged. "So? We've got a few days. I'm sure you'll think of some nice judicious truths for me to tell. Seriously, Germanicus. It's no big deal."

"It is," Germanicus was struggling to keep his tone reasonably level, "because either you are crazy, in which case she is going to have you committed to a nice institution with bouncy walls, OR, there is a hideous supernatural evil lurking in the woods and we have a limited amount of time to deal with it before this woman sics the police on us."

SMALL TIME THIEF

Dr. Applewood's office was not what I expected. There was an austere, almost oriental turn to the decor: bright orange-red boxy benches without arm-rests or any divisions to keep the patients from touching one another. A massively oversized bowl of water sat in the middle of a round coffee table. In the bottom of the bowl there was a collection of variegated smooth stones. A single flower floated aimlessly about on the surface of the arrangement. The obligatory window opened on the waiting room, and the obligatory attendant sat behind it. There was no one, apart from myself, in the room.

"I'm sorry, Miss...?"

"Octavia Kirkman," I said, "I had an appointment for 12:00?"

She looked confused, and then looked at the appointment book and said, in a rather syrupy tone, "I'm sorry Miss Kirkman, but you seem to have confused the time. The appointment is at 1:00, and I'm afraid that Dr. Applewood has already gone out to lunch."

"I'll wait. It's no problem."

"We usually lock the office during lunch hour. There is a cafe within easy walking --"

I held up my crutches. "I barely managed to get up here at all. Is it really a problem if I just sit here and read one of the magazines? I promise I won't touch anything."

The secretary looked slightly worried, but it was not a serious concern. You know the kind of thing, when someone is not actually worried that something bad might happen, but is none the less put off by the knowledge that a rule is being broken.

"Look, I'll tell you what, you have a seat over in the corner there, and I'll see if I can get in touch with Dr. Applewood. Perhaps she can postpone her lunch until later. I'll just pop out and see if I can catch her up." She smiled the slightly unpleasant smile of someone who is doing you a favour which they consider to be disproportionately great, and about which they are therefore feeling disproportionately proud.

"Wonderful," I smiled back and made a show of limping across the room and settling myself down in the corner.

"I'll lock the door so no one can come in and disturb you. Now, I'll be right back but there's a telephone in the office in case anything happens, and there's a fire-escape in the back," she seemed to be under the impression that over the next five minutes a hijacking, a robbery attempt, and several volcanic eruptions were likely to break out in the office. Only one of these things was true.

I waited until I heard the key jingling in the lock and then looked around for security cameras. There weren't any that I could see – hopefully doctor patient privilege was keeping the surveillance limited to the outer hall. Quickly, mustering all of my courage and hobbling at top speed, I reached my hand in through the window and pressed the button that opened the door leading into the office. I crept in, and began to go through the files, trying to figure out the order and find William's before the secretary returned.

If you've never done anything like this, what you will need to know is that time suddenly behaves very strangely. Fear crawls up your back like a rash, pricks of sweat start emerging from every pore, but there is a sort of odd pain that accompanies their emergence, as though the very water in your body is terrified of being exposed to the light. The clock ticks out the seconds at an excruciating pace: time is both hideously expanded, and horribly compressed. To make matters worse, although I had made sense of the filing system, which was straightforward, I could not recall in what year William had disappeared and I was having difficulty doing the basic arithmetic necessary to figure it out.

I started pulling drawers open at random, stopping frequently to listen for the key in the lock. I was formulating excuses in my head, "Oh, I just thought that since you were taking so long I would call and let my brother know where I was," or, "I thought I heard something scuffling around in here. You don't have an infestation of mice, do you?"

At last, I opened a drawer containing weather-beaten, yellowed old files that had been retired long ago. I scanned them, the alphabet slowly trickling out of my mind, and managed to recall that William's file would be under "O" and not "W," and that "O" came before "R." Finally, my eye alighted on it. I reached down and pulled it up. It was small, containing two handwritten sheaves of notes. I then realized my error: I had no bag with me, and I was wearing a skirt without pockets. There was nowhere to hide my treasure. I heard the sound of footsteps in the hall and the jangling of keys.

DO YOU WANT TO CHANGE THE WORLD

"I just went to call my brother to tell him what happened. I fainted. I really don't think I'm feeling that well."

The faces of the secretary and of the doctor hovered above me. I made myself believe the story that I was telling, so much so that their features seemed to swim around like lost fish in a murky pool.

They picked me up and carried me into Dr. Applewood's office. I looked at the ceiling, kind of dreamy-like. The doctor asked me questions that I didn't really listen to, and I said things like "I don't know, it was a long time ago," and, "I kind of feel dizzy; I think it's the codeine," and "Memory is like a mermaid. Very shy." I was careful. I didn't say anything incriminating.

Eventually, I was left alone in the room. I could hear voices out on the other side of the wall, Dr. Applewood arguing with Germanicus about whether I needed to come in regularly. I leaned back against the arm of the sofa and reached, just for a second, inside of my bra. The papers were there, neatly folded, just where I had tucked them. I couldn't wait to get home and find out what they said.

☺   ☺   ☺

"Tell me about the well, William. How did you know about it."

We were outside, sitting around a campfire. Thomas was reading aloud from William's file. He did really good voices: both Doctor Applewood and William sounded creepily like themselves.

"There was a man. He used to take me there. A long time ago. I was only little then, and I didn't know anything about evil. He showed me what to do with the stones. He stood over the Well, and he had his entire hand full of pebbles, and he dripped them down through his fingers. He said that they were tears that had been turned to stone. That they were all the tears of the world. He asked if I wanted to put them into my mouth."

CXXXIII

"Who was this man?"

"He called himself a secret name. He made me put the name into a stone, so that I wouldn't be able to tell anyone what it was."

"Do you know what the name was?"

"Oh yes, I know. But I can't say it. It sticks in my throat. Like when you swallow something that you can't chew. Only the other way around, because instead of not being able to go down this can't come up."

"Did he make you do anything else?"

"He never made me do anything. He only asked me. He said, 'Do you want to change the world? It is so full of sorrows. You can make them go away.' I said I didn't know. But then he showed me a special secret, one of my own, and he showed me how it could go away."

"And what was that secret?"

"My mother never used to love me. But I put it in a stone, and I spit in the well, and now she does. I made it go away. I changed the world."

"I think that your mother always loved you, William."

"Oh no. You think that because you have only ever lived in the world that I've changed. You don't remember how it was before. Nobody remembers how it was. Only me. Because I keep all of the secrets that I've sent away and I'm the only one who still remembers them."

"Do you still meet with this man?"

CXXXIV

"No. I haven't seen him for a long time. He told me that I was going to have to find someone else. In those days I never remembered the secrets. He was just teaching me. He was the one who remembered. Now I'm teaching someone else."

"You mean that you take someone else with you to the well, and you spit stones in together?"

"She has to be very innocent. He said that's very important. If a person has all sorts of secrets and evil in them then they won't work. Eventually, he says that I will have too much evil in me from everything that I have put in the well. It will start to change me. He didn't tell me that until later. He said it would begin to change me, and when it had changed me enough, then I would die."

"Is that why you said that you're going to die soon? Because you believe that you have become evil?"

"Oh, I don't believe it. I don't have to believe. I know that it's true. I used to be a very good boy. Now it's completely different. Now I do terrible things. But I'm not going to tell you about them."

"I think that perhaps you should, William."

"It doesn't matter what you think. I can't tell you anyway. I can do anything, you know. Anything I want. I just do it, and then I put it in a stone, and I put it in the Well with all of the other secrets. Then it goes away. It's like I never did it in the first place."

"What sort of things."

"They're gone out of the world. You can't talk about things that are gone out of the world. There are no words for them anymore."

"And you are teaching this to someone else, you said?"

"A little girl. Soon I'll die, and then she'll have to take over. She'll be the one who takes things out of the world. That's the only thing I'm sorry for. Because when she takes over she will become bad too. I don't want her to become bad. It's just that I don't have a choice."

    ☺   ☺   ☺

Thomas lowered the piece of paper, folded it, and very reverently handed it back to me. "There is no other content. William refused to divulge Octavia's name."

Germanicus fidgeted with a stick that he had stuck into the fire. A few sparks danced heavenward. "All right," he said. "I don't believe in collective hallucinations, and I don't believe that insanity is contagious. Clearly whatever you and William experienced was a real thing. At least in some sense." He was talking to me, but looking off in a completely different direction. "I guess that means I believe you." He fell silent and looked as though this was just about the worst thing that could possibly have happened.

"Good," said Thomas. "Now we all believe the same thing, close enough. The problem is, what do we do about it?"

CXXXVI

THE MOUNTAIN
DEW SCENE

Day six. 12:56 am. The fire is still burning. It's an hour since Germanicus managed to shuffle me off to bed and since then he's already come to look in on me three times. He knows that my leg is broken, and that I can't possibly go anywhere, but he can't shake the paranoid fear that if he looks away for too long I'll disappear again.

"You want a root beer?" he asks Thomas, looking for an excuse to run into the house a fourth time.

"Mmm. Will it be the same kind of 'root beer' that you were drinking on Monday?"

Germanicus looks away guiltily. "Sorry about that..."

"It's okay. I understand. Your parents went away... You had the cellar to yourself... The opportunity to protect your sister's virtue with firearms was too tempting to resist..." The firelight catches in a dimple as Thomas grins.

"Not exactly," Germanicus' face looks pained. "I mean, I wouldn't normally have had that much to drink during the week. But I'd just found out that Sheila – my best friend...apart from you – is pregnant. And her asshole boyfriend is trying to force her to have an abortion."

Thomas nods. Is silent. "So are you pro-life?" he sounds a little surprised.

"Not really. Mostly I'm just anti-irresponsible-losers-treating-my-friends-like-shit."

"Okay. That makes sense."

They fall silent. Thomas gets up and disappears for a few minutes into the woodlot. There's a sound of tree-limbs being hacked by a machete, and he returns with an armload of fuel.

Germanicus realizes he's just zoned out. "Assuming it's regular root beer, do you want one?"

"Not really. I still have Mountain Dew." Thomas raises his can and then throws a piece of wood on the fire. Germanicus' knee bounces nervously and he casts a glance towards the house. "You know," says Thomas, "Hades is not going to come down your father's fireplace to kidnap your sister in her sleep."

"I know. It's just..."

"You're worried."

"Worried enough that I skipped like half my classes this week."

"Whoa," Thomas exaggerates his reaction. "Serious."

The flames flicker around the edges of the new wood, tentatively, like kittens licking a corpse. "That Applewood woman is really suspicious. She thinks I'm lying to her. Which I'm not. The problem is I'm not quite good enough at managing the truth to keep her from noticing that there are gaps in the narrative. And Octavia keeps giving things away without meaning to, and when I try to tell her to be more careful she acts like I'm being paranoid."

"Hmmm. It's very odd that she would think that. Given that she knows you so well."

Germanicus actually cracks a smile. "Alright, so I like my privacy, and I think that writing in secret code is fun. This is different though. We could potentially be in serious trouble."

"I don't think that's what we should be worrying about."

"No." Germancius sighs, "I realize that. But I can think of things to do about the authorities. I can't think of anything to do about a secret well that corrupts the youth and turns the *lacrimae mundi* to stone."

This reminds Thomas. He reaches into his pocket and feels for the stone that we found in the mouth of the skull. He takes it out, holding it up in front of him. It's mostly grey, but shot through with a crystal lattice that captures the firelight, creating the illusion that it is lit from within.

Germanicus reaches for it. "Is that...?"

"Yes."

He seizes it. "Presumably, it holds a secret." He scrutinizes it, turning it over and over between his fingers. "I wonder if there's a way to find out what it is."

"Sure. You put it in your mouth." The stone rises towards Germancus' lips. Thomas' grabs his wrist before he can complete the action. "But I don't think it's a good idea."

There's a moment of tension: Germanicus resisting as Thomas steadily pulls his hand back down. Suddenly, Germanicus lets his arm go slack. He blinks. "Of course. I'm not thinking clearly. I must be tired."

"No. That's not it. Tell me, what was your first impulse when you took the stone from the skull?"

Germanicus thinks back. "I thought...that maybe I should clean it off by sucking on it. I didn't. Because that was clearly just gross. But thinking about it, it is kind of a weird thought."

"Right. It's not exactly the most obvious thing to do. But it was also Octavia's first impulse. And mine."

Germanicus shakes his head, his brows knitting furiously. "I can't believe we're talking as if a stone has psychic powers."

Thomas takes a sip of his drink. "Just figure out what they called psychic powers in Ancient Rome. Then you'll find it easier to believe."

"Seriously though. If it does contain some kind of...whatever...maybe it would be a good idea to find out what it is."

"Maybe. Let's think about it." Thomas thinks by gently scratching his temple with his middle finger. "No."

Germanicus opens his hand ever so slightly. He can see the stone hiding beneath his fingers. It occurs to him that he probably feels about it much like Pandora felt about her box. The thought has way less deterrent power than he would have hoped. "I do get where you're coming from...But we kind of don't have a lot of leads."

Thomas reaches out, pries Germanicus' fingers open, removes the stone and returns it to his pocket. Germanicus blinks, shakes his hand a few times and steals a sip of Thomas' disgusting soda. The oversweet taste of artificial citrus snaps him back to himself.

"Maybe it's best if you hold on to that," he admits. "At least until we figure out what to do with it."

"Probably we should bury it. Tomorrow, maybe."

They go back to staring at the fire. Thomas seems meditative, almost at ease, even though that stone is there right at his fingertips. Germanicus watches his friend stir the coals, and tries to figure out what, exactly, it is that he's feeling at the moment. Eventually he identifies it as gratitude. "Thomas..."

"Yes."

He tries to think of a way to say 'thank-you' without it sounding weird. And fails. "Uh...When you went looking for Octavia, how did you know that she was gone? I mean, how did you know that she wasn't sleeping over at Lydia's or something?"

"I didn't know. You did."

Germanicus considers stealing another sip of Mountain Dew. "No. First of all, I didn't know or I'd have gone looking for her. Secondly, we didn't actually discuss it. As I recall, I mostly just ranted incoherently and you mostly just tried to get me to shut up and go to bed."

Thomas' expression is inscrutable. Eventually, he speaks. "First of all, it is possible to know a thing but to not permit yourself to know. Secondly, the knowledge must go somewhere. In this case, it came to me because our spirits are joined." He glances in Germanicus' direction. "Or had you forgotten about that?"

It isn't something that Germanicus has thought about in years; a ritual that they performed when they were twelve. "Of course I haven't forgotten."

For a moment, they make eye-contact. Germanicus looks rapidly away, aware that he's been accidentally trapped into acknowledging that maybe actually he feels some kind of emotion about his friend. The experience is sufficiently disconcerting that he forgets to point out that Thomas' explanation makes no sense.

"You know," Thomas says after a while, "If you're worried about Octavia, I could take the day off work and stay with her tomorrow."

"Yeah. That would be really helpful. I have a test I shouldn't miss." The small talk almost, but doesn't quite break the tension.

Thomas stands up. The fire is low, it's late, and even though sleep is unlikely it must be tried. They exchange good-nights and then hang around, looking at each other. Something is missing, but Germanicus has no clue what it is. Eventually, out of the blue, Thomas hugs him. Germanicus stands there like a dressmaker's dummy, looking stunned.

"Good-night," Thomas says again. Fortunately, he looks less offended than amused.

Germanicus finally manages to say "Thanks".

I THINK I DROPPED

SOMETHING

"Where are you going?" It was seven in the morning, and I stood in the kitchen doorway leaning on my crutches. My eyes were still sticky from sleep, but I'd hauled myself out of bed because I could hear Germanicus moving around and no way was I going to let him sneak off and play detective all by himself.

"It's Friday. I have class." He grabbed a grapefruit and started slicing it in half.

I looked at him suspiciously. On the one hand, Germanicus was the kind of person who would still show up to school during the apocalypse. On the other, he had just answered my question with a perfectly true statement that implied a specific course of action without specifically stating it. "Class?"

"Yeah. I've already missed a tonne of lectures, and I have a quiz this morning. It's worth 3%."

That did make his story more likely. To Germanicus 3% might make the difference between an adequate grade and a reason to commit hari kari. However, he still hadn't made a clear declaration of intent. "You're sure that you're going to school?"

He took a bite of his grapefruit and looked at me like I was nuts. "Yes... I kind of have to. Look. Thomas promised to come by and look after you this morning. I'll be back around one. I'll even take mom's cell-phone so that you can call me if you need to. I'm sure you'll be fine." He looked at the clock, grimaced, and then squeezed the rest of his breakfast out and poured it into a glass. He gave me a super-quick pat on the head, and rushed out. I went back to bed.

A couple of hours later I woke up to find Thomas sitting in my father's armchair reading one of my father's books. I hadn't heard him come in. "Good morning," he said. "I made you breakfast. I think it might be cold." Sheepishly, he put in front of me a tray containing a plate of pancakes and a cup of tea. I call them pancakes to be merciful: they were more like the tattered remains of something that might have been a pancake in a former life. "They stuck to the pan a little. I'm sure if you put enough syrup on, they'll taste fine."

I took a bite. They were cold, and a little gooey, but he was right. They weren't that bad. "Thanks," I said.

He returned to his chair and sat there in silence, watching me eat. I could see that he was trying to think of things to say, because every so often he would open his mouth a little, but then no word would come out. Finally he said, "Is there anything else that I can do?"

I cricked my neck a little from side to side. It was stiff from lying on the couch all day. "Do you give backrubs?"

He nodded, "Yes." Taking my hand, he helped me to shift down far enough that he could sit behind me. His hands were strong and gentle and he could have been a great masseur except that he was tangibly unsure of himself. "Is that okay?"

"It's really nice. I never get backrubs anymore. Antonia used to give amazing ones, but now she lives in Ottawa, and Germanicus is the worst backrubber in the world. He seems to think that the purpose of a massage is to bludgeon your muscles into submission."

"Well, you let me know if I hurt you."

"Sure." He was working on a spot just between my shoulder blades that had gotten really stiff. Without even meaning to, I let out an audible purr. I could feel his fingers becoming more confident as they dug into the muscle, just enough to get it loose. "You know... I don't think that I thanked you yet for coming and rescuing me."

"It was a good excuse to spend the day in the woods."

"Well, thank you. I was really scared out there, and I kept having these horrible dreams and then kind of half waking up and realizing that I was really badly hurt and all alone." My back was feeling better now. I reached back and took hold of his hands, pulling his arms around my shoulders like a cardigan. I leaned my head back against his chest. "It was nice too, the way you held me to keep me warm. I hope you didn't mind."

"No." I could feel his hands suddenly go clammy, and when I tilted my head back I could see that he was blushing like a beet. I smiled at him upside down. "Octavia," I could see that he was mustering courage. "You..." he came to a full stop, recomposed himself, resumed, "You don't have a boyfriend?"

I shook my head. "I never have. One time I got invited to a party, and we were playing a stupid game where you hid in the dark in a closet with a boy. But when it was my turn one of Catty's dumb friends told the guy to be careful, because he might disappear without a trace. So we just stood in the closet and did nothing. I remember it smelled like shoes."

Thomas laughed and turned a little less red. "I had one girlfriend. She was a Mohawk girl who grew up on the reservation. I would describe our relationship as a mutual attempt at cultural appropriation." Since I clearly didn't understand what that meant, he elabourated, "I dated her because I wanted to get closer to the sweat lodge. She dated me because she liked McDonald's fries."

"How old were you."

"About your age."

That made me feel a little better. Most of the people I knew had already had lots of dates by the time they were sixteen. Even Antonia had managed it behind Mom's back. The only exception I could think of was Germanicus, but Germanicus was obviously weird. I reached my hand up and softly brushed my fingers along the back of Thomas' neck. He smiled, and gently stroked my jaw. We did that for a while, just looking at each other, and then he slid out from underneath me, laid my head back on a pillow, and kissed me. His mouth tasted good, sweet and kind of nutty, and his lips felt nice. It wasn't like in books, where kisses are always fireworks and rip-tides. More like chocolate melting in the afternoon sun. We kissed for a while, and then he laid down beside me, half on and half off the edge of the couch, with his arm around my waist.

We were still lying there like that when the front door opened. Thomas jumped off the couch as though it was on fire, and spent a couple of minutes rearranging his clothes – which didn't need to be rearranged – and smoothing his hair – which just popped back up in all directions anyway. By the time Germanicus arrived at the study door Thomas was bright red again, standing awkwardly in the middle of the room, looking like he'd just pulled his hand out of a cookie jar.

"Hi," Germanicus poked his head in. "I just got back. You guys want lunch?" I nodded. "Okay. I'll go make something then." He closed the door behind him. Thomas covered his face.

"Don't worry," I whispered. "Germanicus is the most oblivious person in the world."

"I'd better go offer to help him." Thomas looked around for a second as though he might have forgotten something, then followed Germanicus out towards the kitchen. I laid back on my pillow, smiling as the warm afternoon breeze drifted in through the window. It was then that I noticed something lying on the floor, just where Thomas had been standing. I reached out and almost fell off the couch trying to get it, but my fingers were just able to touch it. It was the stone. Clearly it had been in Thomas' pocket and had fallen out. I coaxed it across the carpet with my fingertips until I was able to get a firm grip on it, and then quickly scooped it up and hid it in the bowels of the couch just in time. The door opened and Thomas came back in, a slightly worried look on his face.

"I think I dropped something," he said, scanning the floor.

"What?" I asked innocently.

He studied me for a moment, weighing, and I thought that maybe he looked a little hurt. "Nothing," he said. "I'm sure it will turn up."

I'M A FIREFLY

I could barely wait until lunch was over. I could see that Thomas and Germanicus were tense, and whenever they weren't in the study I could hear them furiously whispering to one another. I managed to catch a few scraps of conversation: "...a hole in my pocket. It almost looks burned, as if the stone were burrowing out..." "...if it fell out on the driveway, it's going to be a nightmare..." "...we start looking. What else is there to do?" Finally, I heard them go outside. Quickly, I fished down into the couch and pulled out the stone.

I placed it on my tongue. For a moment there was a taste of mildew and tears, the long-dried spit of a long-dried mouth. I nearly coughed and spat it out but I forced myself to hold it there while the secret that it contained melted into my thoughts. I closed my eyes.

At first I was aware only of the darkness. I blinked, my eyes struggling to adjust. It was a few moments before I recognized where I was. A long arbor of copper trees stretched off into the distance. Several of the boughs held crescent-shaped jewels in shades of blue and gold, and what little light there was glittered in the hearts of these jewels. By it, I could just barely make out the figure of a child standing in front of me. "Hello..." I said with trepidation.

He stepped towards me. I could see that he was very thin, with sunken eyes and a pale, taut face. Someone had dressed him up in a ruffled shirt and a waistcoat, but the clothes were threadbare and stained. "Who are you?" he whispered.

"My name is Octavia." As I identified myself, it was as though a light had come on, a pale, misty light that flooded across the cavern. It took me a moment to realize that the source of the light was me. My body was glowing, and beneath my feet grass began to spring up from the dark stone of the cabin floor. By the light of my own presence, I could see that there were faces peering at me out of the darkness. Gaunt, pale faces with hungry eyes. Some of them seemed to be only toddlers, others were almost as old as me.

The boy who had spoken to me skittered away, but another child, a boy who couldn't have been more than four years old, advanced tentatively towards me. As he stepped onto the edges of the grass his features began to fill out. His eyes slowly brightened, and colour sprang back to his cheeks. Another step and he started laughing out loud, his delicate little mouth chortling with pure delight. The other children began to close in around me, until they were standing in a circle, pressing one another forward into the light, eyes shining, brows bright, their lips rosy and smiling they stood, just out of reach, breathing in the perfume of the flowers and sighing with joy.

"Now children, don't crowd." A figure emerged from the darkness. He had an elderly face, and he held onto a walking cane. An opera cape hung from his stooped shoulders, and his dark suit was shabby but neatly brushed. A small, blond girl in a white lace dress clung to his arm. He made his way through the gaggle of children, pausing occasionally. "Trevor, what's that behind your ear?" he gasped, producing a large, spotted newt which he dropped into the boy's hand. "Didn't I tell you to be careful when you wash. Amanda! You've been letting the bats build nests again in your hair." A small girl's dark braid was lifted, and a tiny winged rodent flew out from under it, hissing in the dark.

He smiled at me and offered his hand. "I am Antonio, and these are my children. I hope you don't find my tricks frightening. A magician can't just produce things from mid-air," he produced a bouquet of copper flowers from nowhere and handed it to a girl of about thirteen, who giggled and hid her face behind the delicate, hammered blooms. "He has to work with the materials at hand." The children looked up at him with obvious adoration.

One little girl threw herself at his leg and clung to it, beaming. "Is the beautiful lady going to stay?" she asked.

"No, *ma petite,* I'm afraid the beautiful lady has a beautiful world she has to go back to. But maybe if you're good, she'll agree to come and visit us once in a while." He leaned down and whispered. "Why don't you ask her for a kiss?"

The little girl came forward and looked up at me with bright blue expectant eyes. I leaned down and kissed her on the cheek.

"Alright now," said Antonio, "you run along and play." The girl who I had kissed ran out into the darkness, but she didn't go back to looking like a ghost. She seemed now to be lit by a kind of inner illumination that spread out from the place where I had bestowed my kiss.

Giggling and rubbing her cheek, she ran around in circles. "I'm a firefly!" she cried out. "I'm a firefly!"

The others looked back and forth between themselves, shuffled forward a little, looked hopefully at me. "Yes, all right," I said, "I'll give you each a kiss." As they came forward I scanned their faces looking, of course, for William. But as the last child turned to skip out into the darkness, now filled with the forms of bright-flitting children dancing in fairy circles and singing unfamiliar rhymes, I had to accept that William wasn't here.

Only Antonio remained standing near me, and the little blond girl who still clung to his arm. "Thank you," he said, and I thought that I could see tears in his eyes. "It makes them so happy, and we haven't had any visitors now in a very long time."

I felt a lump rising in the back of my throat and I blinked back tears. "Where do they come from?" I asked.

"From secrets," he said. A sad smile played across his lips. "Sometimes a mother considers her pregnancy a shame. Sometimes a man wishes that his son never had been born. These things happen. The secrets are sunk into the Well, and the children end up here. I try to keep them amused and happy as well as I can."

"How long..." I asked hesitantly, "How long will they stay like that? I mean, before they go back to being the way they were before."

"It depends," he shrugged. "Sometime only for an hour, sometimes a couple of days. It all depends on the strength of the love that burns in the heart of the one who brightens them." He smiled at me. "I suspect that you have come here with a very great love. Am I right?"

I nodded, my throat constricting as I thought of William. I nodded slowly. "Yes."

"Then perhaps their happiness will linger 'till tomorrow. We may hope."

A slow, creeping anxiety suddenly seized at the edges of my consciousness. It took me a moment to realize what it was: somehow, I knew that Thomas and my brother were coming back. "There are a lot of things I need to ask you," I blurted out. "A lot of things I need to know. But I have to go now. Is it okay if I come back?"

"Please," he said, "it will be our sole delight." He reached out and kissed my hand. When he let it drop, I could feel that something had appeared in my palm. I opened it. It was another stone, identical to the one that we had found in the skull. "I think," he said, "you'll find it easier to return here if you have a second key."

I closed my eyes, reached into my mouth and withdrew the stone.

I was back, lying on the couch, and I could hear footsteps coming towards me down the hall. In my palm, there were two identical stones. I quickly put the original back into its hiding place, keeping the replacement in my hand. When the door opened, I held out the stone with an innocent smile. "I found it!" I said. "It was down in the couch. Thomas must have dropped it when he was fixing my back."

JANUS

"Germanicus?" I rubbed my eyes blearily, "What are you doing?"

It was Saturday morning. My brother had a screwdriver and a mallet and he appeared to be removing the door to my father's study. "I called the parents. Mom's decided that there's evil stalking our house, and she wants me to oil all of the hinges with wolf's fat so that Janus will be more inclined to keep it at bay."

It was hard to sit up. Ever since yesterday I'd felt drained, as if a supernatural torpor was pulling at my soul. I smoothed my hair, which was a tangled mess. "Where do we even get things like wolf's fat?"

"How long have you been a member of this family?"

"Sixteen years."

"And you haven't learned by now that there are questions better left unasked?" He leaned the door against the bookshelf and started dipping the hinge pins into a small clay pot of unctious liquid.

I reached for my hairbrush. "So where did you and Thomas go last night?"

He looked maybe guilty. "Nowhere. Thomas had to go home and take care of his aunt."

"Then why didn't you pick up the phone? Catty called like fifteen million times."

"*Malum.*" Germanicus dropped the pin into the fat and had to go fishing around in it with his fingers. "I just went for a walk. I hope you told her I'd developed leprosy."

"She seemed to think that you'd agreed to take her on a date."

"Ummm. No. I mean, not exactly. I definitely didn't use the word date."

I scowled at him. "I thought smart boys weren't that dumb."

He cast around for something to clean up his hand with, finally settling on his t-shirt which was already pretty badly worn and somewhat stained. "I ran into her in town, and got cornered into apologizing for dumping her in the pond. She very graciously forgave me, and since she forgives me, I'm allowed to make up for it by taking her out. You see how women work?"

I clicked my tongue. "You should never have let her get anywhere near your canoe."

He looked pained. "She wanted to make a memorial to her brother on the anniversary of his death. I could hardly fob her off."

Glaring at him, I burst out, "William is not dead!"

Germanicus looked at me with slightly scared concern. I blushed, angry with myself for having blurted that out. After a moment of awkward silence, there was a knock on the frame of the absent study door. Thomas' face popped into view, his blond hair circling his head like a corona in the sunlight.

"Am I interrupting a moment of important sibling drama?" he asked.

"You're interrupting an important moment of lunacy," Germanicus clarified.

Thomas nodded non-commitally as he stepped into the room. He helped my brother move the door back into place. As Germanicus slipped the well-oiled pins back into the hinges, Thomas moved over and perched himself on the chair next to where I lay. "You know, your sister might be right."

"You mean a ten year old boy might have survived for six years at the bottom of a well with no food, no human contact, no clean water, and no shelter from the elements? Seriously. If he was lucky – or under the circumstances perhaps 'unlucky' is the better word – he died of starvation after 40 days. Probably exposure got him first."

I hated Germanicus and wanted to kick him for being so clinical. The thought of William sitting there, starving, for over a month just made me sick. I glared at him, "I got out!"

He looked a little guilty, but not much. "Viv, if he climbed out, why didn't he come home? He was ten. He couldn't have lived by himself for six years in the woods. If he'd escaped, don't you think he'd have come and let you know he was alright?"

Thomas cleared his throat. "I wasn't speaking in the abstract. Last night, I went to the memorial that they erected to William. I was going to leave a little present for his spirit – one of those spongy styrofoam cakes with jelly in it. I remember he used to always eat those at school. I found this on top of the stone." He handed me a small ornament made of copper wire and stone. It was a butterfly. The workmanship was not quite professional: the wire wobbled a little, and sometimes it wasn't as taut as it ought to have been. Attached to the leg of the butterfly there was a piece of paper, coiled up. I removed it and unrolled it. Written across the paper was a poem:

> *Butterflies are beautiful*
> *But have no depth*
> *Beneath their beauty they are only insects*
> *No different from a beetle or a roach*
>
> *It's six years now since the day I died*
> *Since you emerged from your cocoon*

Feeling butterfly free and light as air

Now you flit to perch atop my tombstone
Drink in the residue of funeral flowers
Neither loving nor hating
You feel as insects do
Only pleasure, and pain.

On the other side of the coil it read, "For Catty." I shuddered and handed it to my brother. "That might be William's writing, but it's older. We were just learning cursive when he went away."

Germanicus handed me back the paper. "If it's a prank," he said, "it's in pretty awful taste."

"I think," Thomas suggested, "Someone needs to talk with Cataline O'Hare."

We both looked at Germanicus. He answered us with mute desperation.

"This is serious," Thomas said at last. "More serious even than your pride."

Germanicus grimaced. "All right, fine," he said. "I'll give her call her tonight."

#OO1

Germanicus Date #001: Debriefing

"So did you liquor her up and get her to talk?" I asked, leaning forward with anticipation.

"She's underage. I took her to the ice cream shop."

I sighed. It figured. "Then she must have known you weren't for real."

"Look, do you want my report, or not?"

"Yes," I said, "I definitely want your report."

This is, more or less, how Germanicus reported his evening with Catty to me. Naturally his version did not have quite so much detail, but I think that mine is more interesting:

It was a muggy day, and Catty's eyelashes looked like they were going to melt in the heat of the sun. Germanicus picked her up at home, very casual. He took Dad's car, and looked to Catty like a suave, sophisticated older man. On the way to the ice cream shop they didn't talk about much. Mostly, Catty talked. She talked about going to school in town, and how she was hoping to get a scholarship abroad – by which she meant the United States. Germanicus bit his tongue and didn't point out that the States is not abroad, but south.

They arrived at the ice cream shop. The old air conditioner chugged away in the window, and Germanicus chose a seat right under it so that they would have to lean their heads in close to hear one another, and so that their voices would not be heard under the masking white noise. He ordered Catty a specialty ice-cream pizza and kept the receipt. "Hey," he said, "didn't you used to have a dog?" It was the first full sentence he had spoken all evening.

"Yes, I did. A Pekingese. That was a long time ago – you have such a good memory!"

"What happened to it?"

"I got rid of it after William died. It was just...I don't know."

"What do you mean...you don't know?"

"I mean, it was a lot of work. Seriously, you had to like stoop down every time the thing took a shit. And I never really wanted a dog in the first place. William was like constantly bugging for one, but he was way too young. Eventually I took pity on him and asked for the dog. And then when I got it, he didn't even like it. He was so weird that way."

"Was the dog in good health?"

She giggled awkwardly. "Ummm...I think so. We sold it to a breeder, so it must have been in good enough health."

"I see. Did it ever get suddenly and unexpectedly sick?"

"I don't think so. Germanicus, why are you asking all these questions about my stupid dog?"

"No reason. Just making small talk. We can talk about something else if you prefer."

"You are so totally shy. Has anyone ever told you that it's cute."

"No. I don't think we can talk about that. Let's talk about the dog again. How did it react to William. Did it like him?"

(He tried in vain to describe the look that Catty gave him at this utterance, but his description was so outlandish that I couldn't recall or believe it.) "Umm...What a wierd question. Though, actually, you know...at first, it was fine with him. I used to let him take it for a walk everyday, since it was him who wanted a dog in the first place. But he used to complain about it, like he was doing *me* a favour. Anyway, after about a week the dog started acting really strange and like yelping and hiding under the couch. Why – do you think that the dog knew he was going to die? That it was precolative?"

"Precognitive. No, that doesn't seem like a very likely explanation. Did you ever think that William was trying to poison the dog?"

"Germanicus...is this a date or are you trying to accuse me of something? Like, I don't even know what."

"Perhaps you knew that your brother was trying to kill your dog. That he hated your dog. Your dog was scared of him, surely you noticed that."

"Why would William be trying to *kill* my dog?"

He leaned back and stared at her, narrowing one eye. "Don't play innocent with me. I know what went down." Germanicus claims that he did not crack a smile as he said this. That he was totally poker faced.

"You are like sick or something. I am totally going home."

Germanicus smiled. "Yes," he said, "I think that would be a good idea."

☺   ☺   ☺

"Germanicus!" I shouted. I wanted to stomp my foot, but it was in a cast and not stompable. "How could you have screwed this up so completely? Were you deliberately trying to be incompetent?"

CLXIV

He smiled, and his poker face cracked. "I'm just pulling your leg," he said. "I wanted to see the look on your face."

"So what actually happened?"

He shrugged. "She has a new dog now. We took it to the park. It peed on a tree. She thought the butterfly was pretty, and that it was weird how it had been left on William's grave. Oh, and apparently I have a cute ass and she wants to see me again."

"Did you show her the poem?"

"Viv," he gave me a look of long-suffering exasperation, "the entire point of my story was to show how these were not really the ideal conditions under which to carry out an interrogation." He shrugged fatalistically. "I did what I could."

I glared at him petulantly for a moment, and then sighed, slinking down into my pillows in disappointment. Germanicus adroitly changed the subject, launching into a rather pointless history lesson on everything he'd learned about the forest and surrounding area during a fruitless trip to the local records office.

If I'd been paying more attention, I would have noticed the sleight of word, how he'd used the false report as a decoy, how it had allowed him to skim over events without telling me a thing. I would have spotted the evasions, and pinned him down. I would have remembered that my brother doesn't consider omissions to be lies.

DEAR DIARY

This is, more or less, how Germanicus reported his night with Catty to Thomas – though I didn't learn of it until much later on.

They were just across the street, sitting out back at Thomas' house. Crickets were singing in the high reeds that Thomas had planted around an old swimming pool which was now home to a school of fish, some turtles, and two ducks. Germanicus had brought along one of the old pipes that used to belong my Grandpa, and he pretended to smoke it, drawing in long drags of cold night air haunted by the ghost of cherry tobacco.

"I really don't know what to make of it," he said, handing Thomas a small, leather-bound book. Across the front, a dozen childish variations on William's signature had been scrawled over and over in black ink. "But I don't want to show it Viv. I think she was in love with him. Possibly she still is. But Thomas, that kid was seriously creepy."

Thomas leafed through the book. "Where did you get this?"

Germanicus blew out a long stream of ghost smoke. "I spent the night with Cataline."

"And plundered her attic while she slept?"

He shook his head. "No. Actually, it's a lot weirder than that."

Thomas took a sip of his ginger ale and waited for my brother to explain.

ⓧ   ⓧ   ⓧ

He had gone to Catty's in the evening following the non-events that he'd described to me. Her parents were away, and she'd served him grilled vegetables, olives and red wine. They spent the evening watching The Shining and discussing the moral and aesthetic qualities of the horror genre. I can only assume that Germanicus did most of the talking, with Catty pretending to hang off his every word. Eventually, she said, "Come up to my room. There's something I want to show you."

Germanicus followed her, a knot of dread forming in his gut. So far the evening had been surprisingly painless. The closest it had come to romance had been when she'd laid her feet across his lap. He'd been hoping that she would drink more, that there would be a brief awkward attempt at seduction, which he'd resist, and then she'd pass out. But she had been behaving with perfect moderation.

Her room was not what he'd expected. It had been stripped of decorations, a plain, almost spartan linen cover was thrown over the bed. There were pinholes in the walls, and residue from sticky-tack, suggesting that there had been other things there before. But now there was only a book-case, a writing desk, and overhead, a series of photographs of boys. Each one was commemorated with a bouquet of dead-dried flowers. She reached into the bookcase and withdrew a leather covered book. "I think this is why you're here." Her face was perfect marble, unreadable, as she handed it to him.

⊙   ⊙   ⊙

"So she had you sussed."

"Weirdly so. I mean, this," he gestured towards the notebook," was the thing I really couldn't have foreseen, but the entire night... the food, the wine, the movie, the conversation, even the way that she'd dressed her room, it was all... I don't know. As though she had no desires or agency of her own. Like she was just a cipher for whatever I might want. And every single one of her guesses was dead on."

"Maybe she's been stalking you on FaceBook," Thomas was joking. He knew how careful Germanicus was about maintaining absolutely no footprint online.

Germanicus strained a smile, "I don't know how she knew. But take a look at this," he flipped open the book to a page written in a childish hand:

<u>My Sisters Dairy</u>

An expiriment to discovr how much of a pursons life can be removd befor they stop to be themselves.

    Materials:
        Catty's dairy
        Stones
        Pen and paper

What followed was a catalogue of days, carefully dated and laid out like a lab report. On each day there was a record of how many pages of Cataline's diary had been copied out while she slept, whispered to a stone and sunk into the Well. "The words disapear. Catty dosn't remember her own thots. This is a very useful finding," William wrote.

Thomas swore. "You're saying that he deliberately tried to strip away his sister's soul?"

"I'm not the one saying it. These are his own words. The rest of his experiments are pretty sick as well."

"And Catty knows of it?"

Germanicus tapped the empty pipe on the arm of the deck chair. "Yeah...she knows."

☺   ☺   ☺

She perched on the edge of her bed, her legs crossed so that the slit at the side of her cream-coloured dress framed the curve of her calf. Expectantly, she waited while Germanicus skimmed through her brother's notebook. Eventually he put it down. "You've read this?" he asked.

She nodded with a soft, light smile. "Let me show you," she went over to the shelf and pulled down a slender volume. It had a cover with bright coloured flowers, slightly faded, and the first entry was neatly dated in a hand edging towards maturity: self-conscious cursive that strove to be copy-book perfect.

October Twelfth, in my eleventh year,

Dear Diary,

That was all. It was followed by two and a half pages, completely blank. The next entry was the same. Germanicus flipped through the entire volume, page after page of diary entries that weren't there. She handed him another diary, the same, and then another. The handwriting became increasingly beautiful as they went, and the entries began to stretch from a handful of pages to five, six, ten.

"I used to write everything in my diaries," she said. "Everything I thought. Everything I felt. Even my memories."

"And you...can't remember any of it?"

She adjusted her skirt so it showed just a little knee. "Not a thing."

"So what does that mean for you?"

She smiled, standing up and taking a delicate step towards him. "That I'm light as air, and butterfly free."

Germanicus could feel cold prickles climbing across his skin, but it was unthinkable to flee. "It doesn't bother you?"

"How could it?" she rested her hand on his shoulder. "I live without consequences. Without worries. I think sometimes I must feel pain, but I just write it down, and in the morning it's vanished away."

He stepped back a little, bumping up against the desk. "You're saying that this is still going on? That it didn't stop when William..." he was about to say "died" but changed the word to "disappeared?"

"It must be, I guess. I don't think about it much." She'd matched him, step for step. The distance between them was closing and there was nowhere, really, that he could run. She rested her other arm so that the back of her hand was just barely touching the nape of his neck. Her perfume circled him, a thick constricting cloud of mandarin and musk.

He took hold of her wrist and removed it from his shoulder. "Catty, I..."

"Don't want to be seduced?" she stepped just a little closer and leaned her forehead against his clavicle whispering, "Do you think I knew everything else, and don't know that?"

He froze. "Okay... Now I'm confused..."

She raised her face and looked up at him, "Imagine," she said, "that you were in my position. Imagine that everything you were had been stolen away. Imagine how important it would be to just be loved."

☺   ☺   ☺

"So what did you do?" Thomas was leaning forward, twisting his straw into a tight coil.

"I hugged her. It didn't really feel optional. Then I tucked her in and went to sleep on the couch." He frowned. "Okay, not actually sleep. She was right there upstairs, and she scares the hell out of me. Mostly I spent the night sitting up and reading that thing, trying to piece out some sort of answers."

"And did you find any?"

"Not exactly. Maybe. I mean... William's experiments were weird and unethical, but they did yield data. I think there might be enough that, given time, I can develop a model for how the Well might work."

WHAT QUALIFIES AS A SECRET?

As I had done about a dozen times over the past couple of days, I reached my fingers into the hollow of the couch and touched the stone to make sure it was still there. There was a slight tingly-electric feeling in the ends of my fingers whenever I touched it. Each time, I considered taking it out and going back to visit and Antonio and the children. Each time, I withdrew. It wasn't that I didn't want to go back but that I was frightened in a way that I couldn't quite explain. At the same time, a dull weight of guilty apprehension had started to build in my gut. It had been almost three days. Even in the absolute best case scenario, it had been long enough that the light had faded and the children were in darkness again. I had to just do it.

My fingers were just closing around the stone when the door started to open. The hinges, having been freshly oiled, were almost silent and I hardly got my hand out of the back of the couch before my brother walked in. "Get dressed," he said. "We're going out."

There had been no previous mention of any outing, and my brother was not the spontaneous type. "Where?"

"I don't know. Thomas apparently has found some little tea shop in the middle of nowhere that he thinks you'd really like, and he says that it's not good for you to have been cooped up in the house as long as you have. So we're going out."

This made the situation clear. Thomas wanted to take me on a date. Thomas did not have a car. Germanicus, therefore, was being brought along as an unwitting third wheel. "Help me get upstairs," I said. "I don't have anything to wear down here."

"I brought you clothes," Germanicus indicated the mis-matched old t-shirt and multi-coloured skirt that he had chosen, seemingly at random, from my drawers.

"Thomas is right," I said. "I haven't been out in a while, and if I'm going to go out I want to wear something nice."

The tea-shop was, as promised, in the middle of nowhere. We followed a series of small, hand-painted signs down a labyrinth of backroads and finally arrived at a small bungalow painted robin's-egg blue. The air inside was rich with the smells of delightful herbal blends and fat, freshly baked blueberry scones. There were about 50 different types of tea to choose from. I selected one that promised rose-petals and lemongrass. Thomas' included all kinds of medicinal sounding ingredients that I'd never heard of. Germanicus ordered coffee.

We took our drinks out to the back garden and seated ourselves in one corner near a shrub that had been sculpted into the shape of a dragon. The entire yard was filled with organic sculptures, trailing flowers cascading out of rusted wheel-barrows, and little hidden copper figures peeking out from under the ivies. Thomas and I tried to make small talk, discussing the merits of various different types of herbs, praising the honeyed beauty of the sunlit day.

Germanicus, however, was visibly obsessing over the problems that we were trying to forget. He had used the honey-pot and some little one-serving peanut butters to build a model of the Well, and you could see his lips moving as he discussed it with some invisible interlocutor. This made it hard to relax. Eventually the conversation ground to a halt and we sat in silence, sipping our tea.

My thoughts drifted. "Do either of you have any secrets?" I asked.

Thomas looked embarrased and hid his face behind his tea cup. Germanicus looked up from whatever he'd been visualizing. "Define."

"Germanicus, don't be a doofus. You know what a secret is."

"No. Actually, it's an interesting question. What qualifies?" He put his cup down and turned so that he was facing the table. "Think about it. If a secret is just a piece of information that you never tell to anyone else, everyone has millions of them. Now, most of them are unbelievably dull, but what's interesting about that is that unless you assume some sort of framework in which the past has an objective existence, outside of human consciousness and memory, then most of those secrets do literally just disappear from reality. For example, I never told anyone what colour my underwear were on the 24th of February 1997. But I don't actually remember the answer to that and it was never recorded anywhere. So the question is, does that piece of information actually still exist in any meaningful sense? Is there a causal trace left on the fabric of the universe by that particular, seemingly trivial choice? If there really were quantum realities, and you could go to another universe where I had chosen a different pair of underwear in the morning, would it have had any impact? You see the implications."

"Of your grotty childhood underpants?" I looked at him incredulously.

Thomas had tilted his head to one side and was obviously considering whatever point my brother was trying to make.

"Don't get lost in the example," Germanicus chided. "The point is, how significant does a secret need to be for it to have the capacity to change the world? And if the Well actually does what it claims to do, how much does the world then change? Is the secret just taken out of memory, or is it actually extricated from the fabric of space-time? And is it taken out completely with all of its roots and its effects, including indirect ones? Or is it a kind of metaphysical hack job that leaves scars that could be found? It makes a huge difference."

I thought of Antonio's children, but of course I couldn't bring that up. "I have no idea. But that's not what I was asking. I was asking if you, Germanicus Kirkman, have any secrets. I mean, real secrets. As in, things you've never told anyone because you're ashamed of them."

He sat back a little, taking his elbows off the table, and considered. "I took a candy once from Harry's store, when I was five."

"A candy?"

"It tasted like soap. I think it was one of those pastel ones that get all sticky sitting in the container because no one will buy them. Probably that's why I stole it. I was terrified that I was going to get caught but I figured that no one was likely to be guarding those ones with any significant vigilance."

"You were five. No way you figured that. Besides, everyone has that secret, only most people stole something worthwhile like a chocolate bar."

He shrugged. "I paid for it. Secretly. I couldn't deal with the guilt, so I went out and walked all around looking at the pavement until I found a nickel that someone had dropped, and then I went in and I quietly left it on the counter when Harry wasn't looking."

Thomas had his mouth covered and was trying not to snigger in a way that suggested that he had way better dirt on my brother than that. "Yes," he said. "And when I was eight years old at camp, I wet my bed. That's the last time I did anything embarassing. Scout's honour." He held up three fingers, and then momentarily crossed two of them before lowering his hand.

Germanicus had the look of a man who's been busted, but still figures it'll be fun to try to wriggle out. "Okay, yes, I do have better secrets than that. But I'm not going to just spill them because – and this is another thing I've been thinking about – they're not just mine. A lot of secrets are shared, there are two or three or four people who know and they're kind of all equally implicated. So the question there is, if you wanted to throw a secret like that into the Well, would you need to get consent from all of the parties concerned? Or would it just be impossible? How absolutely secret does a secret need to be?"

I had to admit that was a good question. "William said that he took the secret of his mother not loving him out of the world. That involved at least two people."

"Yes," Thomas observed, "but it was a lie as well. He said it to gain the doctor's sympathy."

CLXXIX

"Why do you say that?"

"'There are no words for things that have been taken out of reality.' If he had been telling the truth, he would not have been able to tell it."

Germanicus snapped his fingers and pointed towards Thomas. "Yes. Thank you." I could see him fitting another piece into the jigsaw in his head. "However," he added slowly, "on the other hand, it's unlikely that..." he trailed off, as if suddenly realizing that he was walking towards the edge of a cliff. He shook his head. "We need more data points. That's kind of the bottom line. We need more data points, and there's no ethical way of getting them, and even if we could there's no guarantee that we would even be able to remember what they were."

AMID BEAUTY

Germanicus was right. We needed information. But unlike him, I knew where to get it, and I didn't think that there was any moral problem with granting Antonio and his children a little of my light. When we got home from the tea-house, I told Thomas and Germanicus that I was tired and needed to have a nap. Thomas lingered a little, ostensibly to build up my fire but really so he could steal a kiss. Then I was alone. I took the stone out and put it in my mouth.

The world inside the Well slowly faded into view. I was in a slightly different part of it. A thin-limbed child stood next to a machine, staring into darkness as he slowly turned a copper crank. A small pot sat on the floor beside him. There were stones in it, but not that many – it looked like it had once held many more. Every so often the child stopped to drop one of the stones into the hopper at the top of the contraption. There was a grinding, whining sound from the heart of the machine, and a faint glow seemed to be coming from its innards, but if it was producing anything the product wasn't clear.

"Hello?" as I spoke, the light began to seep from my body out into the darkness again. It seemed very slightly dimmer than before, but perhaps there were natural variations, or maybe I had just forgotten how deep the darkness was.

As soon as he saw me, the child dropped the crank and ran towards me, throwing his arms around my chest. "Octavia!" he cried. "You came back!" I kissed the top of his head and he ran back to his work, turning the crank much more swiftly now, with joy.

"I told you she would," Antonio patted the child on his head. He smiled at me. Every time that his expression shifted, all of the lines on his face realigned. It was a fascinating face, full of mysteries. The kind of face I wanted to have when I got old.

Another child ran into view, ran up and furtively kissed the hem of my dress before running off. By the faint light that had suffused her slender limbs, I could now see that she was plucking stones from the limbs of the copper trees.

"You've found our orchard," Antonio gestured around him, "These trees are specially made for the ripening of stones. Little things taken out of your world. Bits of reality that nobody wants. Secrets, supposedly too terrible to withstand the light of day. But many of them include the daylight. They take place in the glorious sunshine, or bathed in the light of the moon. Amid beauty. Terrible and shameful deeds, but committed amid beauty. When we ripen them, the terrible seeds of the secret grow hard and dark inside the stone, but the sunlight, and the rippling of the breeze across the pond, these things age and sweeten. Then they are poured into our light-presses, and we produce these jewels," as if on cue, a small, bright little yellow crystal dropped out of the strange machine. "As you can see, though, the branches of the trees are bare. It is a long time since anyone has sent us any secrets."

"Not since William...I suppose."

"William?" he looked at me strangely. "I'm sorry, I don't know the name."

"But you must!" I cried. "He was the one who taught me about this place. We used to bring secrets all the time and throw them in. And...." I clamped my lips together because I felt I was going to cry. "And one day, when we were giving secrets to the Well he fell in. He must have come here. Where else could he have gone?"

The old man nodded sadly and put a hand on my shoulder. "I apologize. Sometimes some of my children become greedy. Sometimes one of the older children finds a way of contacting a child on the outside, and secures a private supply of secrets. They make their own little distillery. I put a stop to it when I can find them, but I can never bring myself to punish them. They are only children frightened of the dark."

"But...what becomes of the child? The one who brings the secrets in?"

"Did you see him fall?"

I shook my head. "No. I can't remember it really. Not clearly at least."

Antonio's eyes seemed to mirror my sorrow. "There is a rule that I always give to my secret-bearers: you must never bury your own past. Even the secrets of family members can be dangerous, because you bury a little shard of yourself along with the secret, you understand? When it happens to a person only once it's a trivial loss and they recover quickly, like giving blood. But once you start taking your own secrets out of the world there is a temptation to keep on burying your mistakes, to try to perfect yourself by excising every blemish. That's when the moral fibre at the centre of a person starts to crumble. That's when identities are lost. In the end, there isn't enough of the person left to sustain their existence in your world. The Well consumes them and they become a part of her. I'm afraid that is, all too often, what happens when a secret-bearer is not properly prepared. Did your William show signs of corruption before you lost him? Do you know?"

I nodded. "Yes. He said that he was becoming evil, and that when I became the secret-bearer I would become evil too."

"Then I am almost certain of my diagnosis. I will have to find out who was responsible. I am sincerely sorry for your loss." He tipped his hat and began to turn away.

I reached out and grasped the edge of his sleeve. It was wider than it looked, and smooth from having so many things pass in and out of the cuffs when he did his tricks for the children. "Is there nothing... Is he absolutely gone?"

He turned again and answered me only after some deliberation. "Not...absolutely. It is sometimes possible, if the stones where his secrets dwell were gathered together, if the evil were slowly drained from their hearts. My presses have been known to work miracles. Perhaps he could be restored, but it would take a great deal of work and it would demand that I give up a large portion of my harvest. My children would have to go hungry in the dark."

"What if you had a new source of secrets?" I begged him. "I've helped William bring the secrets to the Well before. You could teach me the rules he didn't know, you could train me properly so that it would be safe. I could replenish all of these barren trees," I gestured towards the orchard behind us. "Then your children could have light, and I could have William back."

I looked into his eyes. They were old eyes, and I couldn't fathom half of what they'd seen. "It is costly for the secret-bearer," he cautioned me. "I won't pretend it isn't. We are beggars here, at the table of existence, taking crumbs so that we may have light. But the world is hungry to give its secrets away, it groans with shame and it will try to force upon you more than you can take. You must understand that it can be very painful, and you must have the fortitude to choose which secrets to bear and which to reject. When a secret-bearer is careless, that's when children like mine are lost to the Well. That's when people like your friend lose their souls." He studied me for a moment. "Is that something that you're ready to accept?"

I nodded vigorously. "Yes. If there's any chance of bringing William back, then yes."

He smiled and reached into his pocket, producing a small yellow vial. "I anoint you," he said, pouring a small stream over my forehead, "with the tears of the world and confer on you the offices and duties of Secret-Bearer. Do you accept these burdens, and all that they entail?"

I bowed my head and quietly said, "I do."

STONE.PHT

The first secret arrived at 4:32 in the afternoon, on the 3rd Tuesday in September. The secret was in the form of a box. It was a parcel, delivered by UPS, which is not, as I understand it, the usual form of transmission for terrible and dark doings. Inside of it, nestled in some packing peanuts was an unlabled writable DVD.

I looked at it for a couple of minutes, vaguely afraid that if I played it a trapped phantasm would start to slowly inch its way out of the screen, leaving behind it a trail of sinister goo. I wanted to call Germanicus so that I would have someone to act as a witness in the event that I was pulled into an interdimensional portal to the land of R'Lyeh, but he was out. I put it down on the side table, determined to wait until he got back. I tried to read, but the DVD just sat there, an enigmatic rainbow playing across its surface as the sunlight rippled through the curtains. I couldn't concentrate, and my curiosity was killing me. I opened my lap-top and popped in the disc. It whirred around for a moment, and then a window popped up asking if I wanted to run the movie player. I clicked Play.

On the screen there was a man wearing a mask. There was something strange about the mask: it was one of those traditional happy-sad masks that are supposed to resemble something used in Greek theatre. It was turned sad face up, so that the expression was one of almost comically exaggerated sorrow. For some reason, slightly blurry because of the poor quality of the image, there were two devil's horns sticking out of the side of the mask, in a totally different colour, and apparently made of shiny plastic, whereas the original mask appeared to be pottery.

"This is my secret," the man said, his voice muffled so that it was difficult to make out the words. "When I was five years old, my mother became very sick. I didn't know what it was that she had at the time, but I learned later that it had been cancer. She was in bed all the time, and I resented this. I wanted her to come out and play with me." At this point in the narrative, he lowered the mask. Behind it was another, a harlequin.

"I would go into her room when I was supposed to be letting her sleep. I would creep in and I would go into her bathroom cabinet and pull out her make-up. She was on some sort of drugs so that she didn't wake up. Then I would paint her face to look like whatever I wanted. I made myself so many perfect mothers that way. Sometimes I would take dresses out of her closet and drape them over her body and I would hold conversations with her. I was always careful to clean up afterwards, before the nurse came to check on us." He lowered this second mask, behind it was a third, a weeping porcelain face with stars around the eyes.

"She died eventually. I went into the room where the corpse was. I didn't really understand what it meant for her to be dead. I snuck upstairs and I got the make-up and decorated her. I thought that if I painted her the right way then she would come back to life." The face lowered again, and this time it was replaced with the plastic devil's face.

"When she didn't wake up, I became desperate. I started praying and praying for her to rise from her bed, but she didn't. I had heard in a movie that I was not supposed to have watched that you could sell your soul to devil. I sold mine so that my mother would wake up."

The final mask was revealed: a cut-out of a blown-up photograph of a woman's face, with puffy eyes and thin, stretched, painfully grey skin. There was a hole where the mouth ought to have been. For the first time, I could see a little of the man behind the mask: just a fringe of short brownish hair. Nothing that would give away an identity. "She didn't sit up, but now I often wake up in the morning with my face covered in make-up, and one of my mother's old dresses stretched out over me. I know that she has come in the night and lived in my body."

Abruptly, the screen went dead. When I turned it back on, I found that the video-player had crashed. There was only one file on the DVD called "stone.pht" which was not a real extension, or at least not one that I'd ever encountered, and clicking on it just produced an error message. I ejected the DVD and put it in again, but the computer insisted, rightly enough, that it did not recognize the file type. I had no idea why it had ever played in the first place.

ACT III

IN ILLO TEMPORE

In the Beginning there were the waters. Every mythology agrees on this. Before the God of light and fire, of sky and spirit comes to impose order on the world there is the uncreated void. Inanimate matter. Water and stone.

It is a story of primeval enmity. Maybe the sky god forces himself on the goddess of water and earth and she brings forth men and monsters that make war for all time. Maybe the god of light wrestles with Leviathan in the depths and slays her on the point of his spear. Maybe the spirit of God broods over the waters and cries "Let there be light." And then the stars burst forth, piercing the womb of the void. But the chaos resists this and seduces the stars so that a third of them turn on heaven and become bringers of destruction. Uncreators. Servants of the void.

CXCV

Here's how I think it happened in illo tempore. The world had not yet been made. In the eye of the Creator, the fields were filling with animals and men. The dews of the first waters were washing across the newborn blades of grass. The tube worms were opening their mouths to drink in the heat of oceanic springs. But this was the time before time, when things did not yet exist. When all Creation was being thought of, conceived and ordered in the Creator's mind.

He stopped for a moment to confer with Himself. The conference concerned the creature He called man. On the vast plateau of His imagination, all of the human civilizations were lined up in ranks. There were many that you and I wouldn't recognize: an armadillo in armour made of seashells, a bright blue lion weilding a spear with a wickedly curved point. Others we know well: the Roman Eagles, the Coeur-de-Lion, a Chinese dragon with a high plumed brow. They were all set in place like armies on manoeuvre, ready to be marched out onto history's battlefields, to fight, and gain their victories, and die.

During the day they stood to attention, all turned towards the face of God. But then night fell. Tricksters began to climb out of the woodwork. Maybe it was a serpant. Maybe Loki. Perhaps Raven came. They showed the minds of men a terrible thing: that for all of their nobility and all of their acheivements, one day, they would be judged.

Then the spirits of the ages waited until it was completely dark, until even the eyes of heaven might be blind. Then they came together in a secret place. Each one had clutched in its claws, or its talons, or its teeth, a stone. The surface of each of these stones was pocked and scarred and marked with a thousand transgressions, secret evils, briberies, unjust rulings, mock trials, slave mines and concentration camps. Children slain and enemies massacred. Innocents sacrificed to satisfy dark gods.

Then they began to dig, tooth and claw, sometimes even gouging one another's flesh in their frenzy. They dug a hole in the foundations of the earth, all the way down to beneath the firmament, down to the void.

The waters at the bottom of the Well were older than the glaciers. Older than the rains. Older than the first molecules of hydrogen and oxygen. Older than the forces that made the first atoms coalesce. The Well reached down into the primordial and uncreated waters, to a place that had never been breathed upon by the divine spirit nor touched by light. It could dissolve anything and from its nothingness anything could arise.

So the spirits of the ages brought the stones that contained their secrets and placed them in a circle around the hole. Their sins made a tower, reaching almost up to the sky. At the end of the world, when the last night fell, they would all come and push on those stones until they all went tumbling down into the abyss to be hidden from the eyes of judgement.

When they had finished with their work they went back and polished their standards. They pressed their uniforms and mended their flags. Then they stood to attention again. Their hearts were satsified and they thought, "Now we are safe."

But the Creator is not so easily cheated. The Well was made to hold the horrors of history: the genocides and holocausts, the rape of cities and the murder of sons. But concerning such things God could not be deceived. And so, like so many of the works of men, the Well diminished. It was lost and forgotten until almost no one knew of its existence. It became a sunken hole where the shabby evils of ordinary men could be squirreled away.

Thomas stopped reading and placed the page in front of him on the ground. "I can't prove a word of that," he said. "It might be nothing more than my imagination running wild. Visions are dangerous that way. But you asked me to take this to the lodge and pray about it, and this is what I saw."

PARAONTOLOGICAL

PHENOMENA

"Great," said Germanicus. He shrugged and his lips thinned as he looked in my direction. "There you go, Viv," he said, "you ask for visions, you get visions. Now let's get down to what can actually be proved."

He produced a notebook and laid it down on the kitchen table. It was covered in completely incomprehensible sigils, Germanicus' private code. Rumour was, you would have needed a team of experts and a military computer to decrypt it. Fortunately, Germanicus converted it to something like English as he read.

We're dealing here with a set of phenomena that I'm going to refer to as "paraontological," that is, they exist alongside being as such, and in some cases interact with it, but their actual status vis a vis existence is difficult to discern.

These facts are known. When a secret is removed from the Well it is forgotten. No one remembers it anymore except for the secret bearer. It is, however, possible for the secret-bearer to talk about secrets that have been removed from the world provided he does not specify their contents: e.g: if a secret concerning birds is removed from reality, the fact that birds are involved may be noted. The nature of the experiment can also be recorded, in this case, "I reminded Vivi that we had done this the day before. She did not remember the events." However, we are unable to reconstruct what, precisely, happened to the birds. Ergo, it would seem that all facts uniquely pertinent to the secret itself cannot be spoken once the secret has been removed. I note, as an overall tendency, that the moral content of the secret seems to be its most involiable aspect.

Secrets do not, however, have to concern any direct evil, or indeed any events which are loathesome or undesirable to their source. It seems unlikely that the direct permission of the source is required in order to remove secrets from the world, however, this is not known. William makes no record of any attempt to seek Cataline's consent, however her statements post factum suggest that her consent may have been possible to obtain. Unfortunately, there are significant ommisions regarding methodology in the extant texts.

One of my initial suspicions seems to be confirmed by the evidence: that the removal of secrets is imperfect. Cataline recalls her dog being frightened of William, and William records that the dog seemed to demonstrate emotional reactions commensurable with events that had been removed. He reports that several forms of violence were attempted against the dog, and that in all cases physical evidence of the injuries was entirely absent after the secrets had been drowned. The dog, however, reacted to his presence with growing fear. The precise mechanism at play here is not known. Several possibilities might be entertained, but without further data none can be preferred.

We are able to confirm that the following effects are possible: objects created during the course of a secret may be destroyed, objects destroyed during the course of a secret may be restored. Injuries inflicted will be healed. Death, in the case of animals at least, may be reversed. Social consequences are more ambiguous, and almost impossible to judge. I can, for example, think of several times that I felt a specific distaste towards Cataline O'Hare in the weeks preceding William's dissapearance, with little to no direct provocation that I can recall. However, it could be that a) I entertain strong prejudices against popular girls who I perceive to be callow, unintelligent and promiscuous, or b) that this is an example of confirmation bias on my part. Direct social consequences, such as school detentions or legal investigations are, however, obviated by the removal of the actions they address.

As for the status of secrets once they have been removed, I wish to analyze in detail one experiment in particular. William records that after school one day he snuck into the kindergarten class, crushed the skull of the class hamster, and then hid the body in the desk of one of the children. That evening, before the crime would be discovered, he threw it into the Well tucked into a stone that he had specially prepared for the purpose by wrapping it around with a long piece of twine. The next morning, the hamster was still alive and the class was undisturbed. He returned to the Well that night and removed the secret, bringing it back into the world. The following day the class was in a state that must fairly be described as traumatic confusion: the pupils were greiving the violent death of their pet, and the child in whose desk it had been placed insisted on being moved to a different seat. However, nobody could clearly recall the events of the previous day when the hamster's death had been discovered. An investigation was underway, but when questioned the investigators couldn't say who they had interviewed or what they had learned. William then returned the secret to the Well, the hamster resumed living and the class continued as before, however the students became visibly agitated and confused if questioned about the events of the previous day. Finally, he removed the stone again in order to obtain the freedom to report on these events in full.

He notes that on this final removal the death of the hamster rose to the level of a schoolwide emergency, that the kindergarten class seemed to be in a state of collective shock vastly exceeding what one would expect four days after the death of even the most beloved of animals. The staff also exhibited an almost hysterical concern. William records being frightened of his role in the crime being discovered, and laments that he may have to "ruin" the experiment by removing it again from the world. One suspects that although he recalled the secrets he had buried, William found it difficult to think about them clearly without writing down his thoughts.

I report this experiment in detail because it particularly illuminates some of the metaphysical questions raised by the existence of the Well. Specifically, it suggests that the Well is not a mechanism for producing "alternate realities" or for moving subjectivities between "quantum universes," assuming that such things are cosmologically possible in the first place. New causal pathways do not emerge to repair the damage to the fabric of the world. Rather, reality seems to become "threadbare" as it were in *places where peices have been removed. One thinks of a dropped stitch in a knitted garment. This suggests that on careful analysis, the gaps could be discovered.*

The long-term effects of this experiment on the kindergarten class and teachers are striking as well. Although William could not have known this, school records indicate that a very high proportion of students, and several staff members, had to be referred to counseling after the events. The incidence of serious mental disturbance appear to wildly exceed that which would be expected in the case of the death of a class pet. Among those students whose medical records I was able to obtain, I found that there was a significant rate of on-going mental trauma, exceeding normal rates of mental illness in the general population by a factor of 16%. Acknowledging that this is an extremely small sample size, and that therefore the margin of error is quite high, the data still suggests that the removal of secrets may have long term mental health sequelae for those involved. I would hypothesize that treatment in such cases would be particularly difficult, given that the underlying events cannot be accessed either by the subject or his doctor. This hypothesis would demand further study, which cannot be pursued due to ethical constraints.

"Germanicus," I interrupted. "Is there any chance of you telling us the rest of this in language that people actually understand?"

"I composed it in Latin, and I'm both decrypting and translating on the fly. I think I'm doing pretty well. Besides, you asked for a report." Full stop, for emphasis. "This is a report."

"I think she meant the Globe and Mail, not The Annals of Postmodern Cosmology," Thomas said.

Germanicus scratched his ear. "I've really just been laying down the groundwork. I haven't even gotten to the heavy metaphysics yet."

I groaned. Thomas suggested that he summarize for me.

"Uh. I guess the upshot is that I don't really know what the Well is, or how it works, but I have some interesting theories..."

"And some interesting sources," I shot him a dirty look, "I couldn't help but notice that there are some 'significant methodological ommissions' in your text." I didn't know where he'd gotten his information from, but it made me mad. William would never have done those things.

"Um. Yes. In the interests of fostering mutual trust, I figured I'd better come clean." He reached into the book bag that slumped against his chair. "I may not have mentioned that Catty gave me this." He handed me William's notebook. I grasped it with hungry hands, my fingers searching out the curves of the beloved signature that the pen had etched into the leather surface of the book. As I looked up, just for a moment, I thought I caught of look of disappointment on Thomas' face. Germanicus continued, "I don't think you'll like what it contains, but given the perils of keeping secrets from one another I thought you'd better know the truth."

THE BRD
XPIRIMINT

For a moment, just a moment, Germanicus' confession struck my heart and I even considered telling him about Antonio and the secret that I'd received the day before. The moment the thought arose in my mind I realized that it was stupid. Germanicus would no way understand. I put William's notebook down on the oak surface of the table, flipping it open. The shade on the overhead lamp cut a line of light and shadow across the middle of the page.

"Thanks." I pretended to be more offended than I was. I didn't want Germanicus to be suspicious that I was keeping secrets of my own.

"You know," Thomas said to my brother, "I would be interested in hearing your theories. And I think maybe Octavia would like some time."

I smiled, and tried to make it a nice smile, but on some level it bothered me that he had to be so considerate. I knew he was jealous of William. So why was he so quick to let himself be pushed aside? "I really would appreciate that," was what I said.

As Thomas and Germanicus headed towards the games room I flipped through the book. Mostly I wasn't reading. Mostly I was just feeling the pages that William had touched, remembering his little turns of phrase, the earnestness with which he had pursued his life. There was one page, though, that sent a kind of chill running down into my bones. It was titled "The Brd Xpirimint," and it was the first time I had seen my name in the book.

I read, and as I read I began to reconstruct a memory.

It happened about a week before William died. He took my hand and led me away from the playground during school. I'd never skipped school before and I could hardly believe that I was doing it now, but there was something in the way that he looked: deadly serious, as if he wouldn't be able to bear it if I said no.

We waited until the lunch supervisor had her back turned, then snuck out past the playground equipment, to the hole that the big kids kept making in the wire-mesh fence, and ducked through.

Our elementary school backed onto a big empty field where corn used to be grown, the sort of field that still keeps the edges of its old shape but where all the plants are just big, sprawling, wasteland weeds with tough old stems.

William and I traipsed out into the field and he led me along to the edge of a river. It wasn't a real river, no more than a seasonal creek, but it seemed like a river to me. We bent down at the edge and he drew my attention to something that was resting in the crook of the root of an old tree stump. It was a nest. In the nest, there were five beautiful eggs. "Watch," said William.

I had never remembered what happened after that. Not until tonight. The words in the notebook seemed to have disturbed the past, and images were bubbling up, slowly, like air trapped in a porridge pot.

William reached down and picked up one of the eggs. He held it to my ear, and I could hear something inside of it, disturbed by our presence. From nearby, I could hear the screech of the mother bird, suddenly realizing our intrusion. She flew towards William, pecking feverishly at his hand, but he swatted her aside. She was only small. Small and brown and helpless. William put the egg down on a rock and crushed it with his palm. The little bird inside crawled out, its body featherless and goopy, its little beak opening and closing piteously as it tried to cry. The desperate mother flew at William again, fearless in her desire to protect her eggs.

"Stop!" I grabbed William's hand as he reached again towards the nest. "Stop this. What are you doing? Those birds are too little to be hatched."

"Watch. Watch and see if you remember." He picked up the remaining four eggs and crushed them all together in his palm. The bloody yolk ran down his fingers, the bones of the baby birds cracking as easily as their shells. He dropped them in a pile; a bloody, yellowy mess. "I did this yesterday," he said. "Do you remember that?"

I had started crying. I couldn't understand why he was doing this. "You never," I said, "You never did anything like this before."

"Oh yes. I did it yesterday. And you cried. Just like today. I'll do it again tomorrow, if you like. Just so you can see how you don't remember."

"I'm telling!" I shouted, tears streaming down my face. "I'm going to tell the teacher what you did!"

"No you won't," he grabbed my skirt so that I couldn't run away. "If you do, I won't help you bring them back to life. We can make them okay again, you know." He smiled. "It's an experiment, to see about bringing back the dead. It could be very important. It could save lives."

I wiped my nose on my sleeve and dried my eyes. "Promise," I said, "that you won't do it ever again?"

He tilted his head to one side. "I promise," he said, "if you remember this, I won't do it again."

☺   ☺   ☺

I hadn't remembered, not until now. I snapped the book closed. My stomach was churning and I wanted to throw the pages in the fire. Reminding myself that it wasn't William who had done these things, I took a few deep breaths and lowered my head onto the table. William only began to perform such experiments after the secrets had started to unravel him, after evil had wormed its way into his heart.

I could feel the weight of the secret that I carried, a leaden canker that I needed to spit out. When William had carried these burdens he had been so young, and there had been nobody to warn him about the dangers. I understood though the need to be strong, to gather these fragments until William could be put together, whole.

A GHOULISH PASTE

It was the middle of the night. I had gone to bed a long time ago, but now there was a weird kind of chill coming into the room. I blinked several times, opened my eyes. It was one of those nights where the clouds catch the moonlight and spread it like a ghostly pall over the world. I could make out the familiar shapes of my father's study, but something felt wrong. I flicked on the little bedside lamp.

Everything seemed in place. The armchair tucked into the corner next to the fireplace, the little statue of Romulus and Remus suckling from the wolf, the coat-stand in the corner with my father's collection of umbrellas. It was all very familiar. It took me a moment to realize what was wrong. The door leading out of the room was not my father's. It was supposed to be old oak, varnished to look like a dark hard nut. Now, instead, there was a bifolding door with wooden slats and a chipped corner. I got up and walked over to it, stepping easily as if my leg had never been broken at all.

I opened the door. Inside, there was a rack of men's suits: a blue one, badly creased, that looked like it had not been worn in years. A couple of smart pin-stripes. A black wedding suit in a cellophane bag. A small ironing board folded down from the inside door-jamb, and some sort of miracle steaming device lay abandoned on the floor. From the top shelf, a box labeled "Electronics" was spilling out its innards over the edge of the shelf, wires and old controllers snaking down into the interior of the closet and tangling with hangers.

To one side there were four large garment bags of the old-fashioned type: made out something that resembled thick shower-curtains. I reached out and picked one up and unzipped it. Inside was a dress, a pink party dress that looked like it had been tailored sometime in the 1950's. It had a wide skirt, and the neat stitchwork of a careful amateur seemstress. A wavy margin of white trim circled the neckline, but it was peeling back in places and I could feel the stiffness in the fibres, the hardening and crackling of old lace.

I took the dress off its hanger and brought it back into the room, laying it on a wardrobe that had appeared along the west wall. I sat down in front of the mirror and reached guiltily down into the bottom drawer. A pile of innocent looking manilla envelopes were nestled there on top of a springy file-folder full of old bills. I picked this up. Underneath it, there was a jewelry box. I opened it and removed several cosmetics: bright purple lipstick, green eyeshadow, clumpy mascara with silver sparkles in it. With clumsy strokes I caked ghoulish smears of paste over my face. Then I put on the gown.

As soon as I was dressed I felt that I had changed. An old song, so familiar it made me ache, was playing, low at first, scarcely heard, like it was coming from down the hall. As it got louder I began to whirl around the room, dancing, dancing, with a terrible urgency, frenzied. I was starting to get dizzy but I wanted so badly just to dance. A weird kind of pain was spreading up into my torso, but the pain seemed to belong to a different body, someone far away. All I wanted was to dance, and dance, and dance.

"Octavia!" Someone was shouting from a great distance. The name sounded familiar. Wasn't she Nero's wife? Poor girl. I seemed to remember she'd had an unhappy end.

"Octavia!" It was the same voice again. My arm slammed into something, and then someone grabbed my shoulders. There was no-one there. A shadow. I pushed them away. Why wouldn't they let me dance?

"Viv! Listen to me!" The shadowman grabbed me harder now, around the waist. Everything seemed dark and strange. I tried to kick, but my leg felt like lead. Screaming, clawing at my assailant, I kicked with the other leg. There was a shooting pain, and I toppled to the ground. The figure hovered over me, his hands seizing my wrists and pinning me to the floor. I struggled for a moment, and then, realizing that it was futile, I let myself go limp. Whatever he was going to do to me, I hoped it would hurt less if I didn't fight.

"Viv?" The pain was starting to become more intense, and the voice... I still couldn't place it but it seemed like it might be someone I knew.

"Where am I?" I said.

"You're in Dad's study."

I blinked a couple of times. I was so dizzy. The world was spinning, and the pain was becoming a lot more severe. "It hurts!" I whimpered. "Why does it hurt?"

"Because you've been spinning around like a whirling dirvish. On a broken leg."

"Ow." The room slowly started to right itself and I realized where I was. Germanicus' face – it's not that it became clearer, more that the identity associated with it slowly faded in. "OWWW!!! Germanicus, it really, really hurts!"

"Stay here," he said. "I'll get your morphine." I tried to roll over into a more comfortable position but it only made things worse. I curled my fingers around the feet of the armchair and held on tight, as if maybe I would be able to pull myself out of my body and escape from the pain.

After either a second or forever, Germanicus returned. I grabbed the bottle out of his hand and took a swig. It seemed like probably about a teaspoon. As I laid my head back on the carpet he took the bottle back and read the dosage information printed on the front. A look of concern creased his face, but I didn't care. The pain was subsiding, far far away and as I waved good-bye to it a giggle started to build up deep inside. Soon I began to laugh, loud and high and free. It was just so funny to not be in agony.

Germanicus lifted me and I could see that he was struggling to get me back onto the couch. He was like super, super tired. I laughed even harder, tears rolling down my cheeks. He disappeared again, then reappeared like a cuckoo-clock bird. He had a wet cloth that he was for some reason wooshing around my head.

My brother asked me a thing.

So I explained, words gushing out of me like pink water from a giant Barba-Papa balloon. I felt like ice-cream.

We both slept deeply, but uneasily. Germanicus was slumped in Dad's arm-chair, his neck crooked at an unnatural angle, his cheek smooshed up against the wing. I lay half on, half off the couch. At some point in the night it had seemed reasonable to try to go to the bathroom but I had abandoned the project two steps in and only part of me had made it back to bed.

My face was a whorl of smeared colour. Oranges, purples, greens, a kaleidoscope drawn on in Crayola ink. My brother's exhausted attempts to wash my face had only succeeded in spreading the stain down onto my cheeks, the ink running like carnival tears.

MUTINY
ON THE RHINE

Germanicus was awake, stumbling around and tidying up my father's study in a haphazard, inefficient way. You could tell that he hadn't slept much because he kept getting distracted by increasingly irrelevant details – like right now he was using a sewing needle to scrape out years of accumulated greasy crud from the tiny brass ridges on the switch for the desk lamp. I watched him for a few minutes and then asked if he could bring me some pain-killers.

"Not until after you've explained what happened last night. I don't want to be mean about it, but I do actually need an account that doesn't sound like it's being delivered by a pack of hyenas."

"I was asleep." I told him the truth just like he had taught me to: judiciously.

"So you have no idea why you were drawing all over your face and dancing in your sleep on a broken leg?"

I swallowed. "I guess I was having a dream."

His expression hardened. He put down the sewing needle and turned his full attention to me. "Your account last night was incoherent, but it did contain some valuable key-words. So we are going to start again, and you are not going to lie to me."

"What key words?" I asked. I couldn't really remember what I had said.

"This is *not* a game, Octavia. Do you have any idea how stupid and dangerous it is for you to be keeping secrets from me right now?" He seemed angry, like genuinely angry.

"Oh, like you never keep secrets from me? What about William's book? You kept that a secret. You even lied to me –"

"I didn't lie. I was very careful about that."

"Call it what you want, but you didn't tell the truth. And you still haven't told me how you actually got it off of Catty."

"She just gave it to me. That's all. And also, I shouldn't have kept it a secret. And I admitted that as well. Furthermore, if you try to change the subject again, I will..."

he stopped, closed his eyes. His mouth was set like stone, and I couldn't tell whether he was trying to think of a suitable punishment or whether he had several in mind and was resisting the urge to execute them summarily. "Don't fuck with me. I want the truth."

I'd never heard my brother swear, not in English, definitely not to me. "First of all," I said, "I'm going to tell Mom that you swore. And second--"

"You're going to do what?" he was almost yelling now, and he'd stood up, steadying himself on my father's desk.

"You always pretend like you're so perfect. You never lie. You never swear. You've never kissed a girl. You've never --"

"You know what I've definitely never done? I've never put my life in danger chasing after some stupid, creepy dead kid who's been gone for over six years!"

"He is not dead! And he's not stupid. And he's not creepy! He was never like that. It was the Well that made him that way, and maybe you think that you'd do a hundred million times better than he did, but you know what Germanicus, you wouldn't. Because you're just as flawed as everybody else. And if you knew the first thing about what love is --"

"Octavia, you have no idea. Love is not some stupid kiddie-pool infatuation *cum* adolescent obsession. Whatever idiotic feelings you have for William, they're not it."

"Oh, and you would know Mr. 'I don't have time for the fair sex until I'm done my PhD.' Mr. 'I'm not that stupid, but, oh wait, I kissed Bratty Catty, actually, but don't tell Viv.'" I looked at him triumphantly, waiting for a moment of vindication that wasn't going to come.

Instead, he started laughing. The laughter dissolved, after a couple of moments, into something that resembled nervous sobbing. "I can't... I cannot believe you're this stupid. I honestly can't. I really, really hope that this is the Well starting to corrupt you, because otherwise..." He turned his back to me, looking out the window. After a minute, he turned around. His face was perfectly calm, and was somehow scarier because of that. "Octavia, I want you to listen to me. Either you tell me, right now, why you were clomping around at midnight or I quit. I will walk out. I will unplug the telephone, and drive to school, and get on with my life, and you will lie here without painkillers, without anyone to bring you water, or food, or help you take a shit, or drive you to the hospital the next time you do something demented."

"You wouldn't dare. You wouldn't dare because then everybody would know that your so-called virtues are just a facade. That really you're just arrogant and mean."

He opened the drawer of my dad's desk and withdrew a pair of heavy shears. I gave him a "Yeah, right," look, which he ignored as he unplugged the telephone and cut off the cord. He folded it double and slung it behind his back, Centurion style. "You think I'm bluffing? I don't bluff.

Ask Juvenal. He will confirm that Germanicus Kirkman has his limits, and that you do not want to see what happens if you push me past them."

I glared at him. He was of course bluffing. No way was he going to abandon me. "Leave," I said. "Leave if you like. But remember that I climbed out of a well all by myself with a broken leg. Remember that I can be way more determined then you think. If you leave, I *will* get to a telephone. And I *will* call Mom and Dad. And I *will* tell them --"

"That you broke your leg out in the forest where they expressly forbid you to go? While skipping school? You're going to tell them that? Go ahead." He sat down in the arm-chair, folded his arms and waited.

I grabbed my crutches, heaved myself to my feet, swung my leg forward. A terrifying bolt of pain surged up into my hip, and I collapsed on the floor. I lay there, crying as much in frustration as in pain.

Germanicus did nothing.

"Help me!" I ordered him, angrily.

He cleared his throat. "Do you remember, the mutiny of the Legions on the Rhine?" The question was rhetorical; he barely paused. "Germanicus," he was speaking of the general for whom he was named, "was sent to restore order. He sat and watched while the mutineers were thrown down to be cut to pieces by their comrades. And then, to restore the glory and the honour of the Legions, he led a massacre of the Germanic tribes." Now he paused, for emphasis. "Women and children were not spared." He picked up his tablet and tapped hard on the screen. "Don't imagine for a moment that my 'so-called' virtues extend to the sentimental."

I lay there whimpering while my brother sat impassive, pretending to be some stupid Roman prince. After a long time I managed to drag myself back up onto the couch. I lay, staring at the ceiling, my fists clenched in hatred. "Fine." I reached behind the cushions and pulled the stone from its hiding spot. It occurred to me that the truth would hurt him way more than my silence would. "This is the stone that Thomas dropped," I planted it on my brother's knee. "And I know what it contains."

He laid the tablet down as though it were a testament of judgement. "I'm listening."

"I've found William," I said. "And he is alive. And I'm going to save him."

"How?" He seized the stone.

I explained about Antonio, and what he had promised. I explained about sacrifice, and love, and the joy that I had given to the children in the Well. Germanicus stood up and began to pace, grinding his fist against his hand. I could see that he was losing his footing on the moral high-ground, and it felt good to finally see him fall down. Then I explained about the DVD that I had received in the mail, and why I had been dancing, and how we had to get the secret to the Well so that I wouldn't dance again. That's when he lost it.

CCXXI

"I can't..." Germanicus pulled his fist out of the hole that he had just made in my father's study wall. "I just can't... I can't believe that you would..." He stopped, staring down at the broken plaster.

"You need to calm down," I said. "You're making a mess."

He turned and glared at me. "This is me calm." He punched the wall again, managing to bloody one of his knuckles on a screw, "This is me controlling my passions as much as is humanly possible."

My leg was really hurting, but I didn't dare say anything about it. We locked eyes. No way was I backing down: I could be just as Roman as him.

The door swung open on it's well-oiled hinge, "And this is a coffee that you could probably really use." Neither of us had heard Thomas come in, but I was super glad to see him. I knew I could get him on my side. He extended a mug towards my brother.

For a moment, Germanicus looked at the cup like it was a dead rat. Then he grabbed it, removed a large bottle of brandy from the liquor cabinet, and poured a hefty slug into the rich, dark brew. He took an overlong swig from the bottle before he put it away.

"Do you think that's wise?" Thomas seemed pretty sure it wasn't.

Germanicus took a gulp of coffee. "Wisdom has left this house."

"Okay." Thomas gave me a sympathetic look. "So you've decided to wage war on the drywall?"

I could see that my brother was finally trying to pull himself together so he wouldn't look bad in front of his friend. "Thomas, you have no idea what she's done. You have no idea how stupid she's been."

"I'm not stupid!" I lost my temper. "If you were in my place you would have done the same!"

He gave me a look as if he might actually be contemplating murder. I shut up and looked at Thomas, a helpless, forlorn look that communicated that I was in need of aid and that my brother had gone insane.

Thomas put a hand on Germanicus' shoulder, tentatively, as if he were a wounded animal. "I think we need to go and talk. Outside. You should leave your coffee here."

"And leave her alone? No. No way. It isn't safe."

"I'm not sure it's safe for you to stay here... It seems like your equilibrium may have been disturbed."

My brother was breathing heavily, desperately trying to bring his passions to heel. "Fine. I'll go for a walk. Probably that's a good idea. But you have to stay and make sure she doesn't do anything stupid while I'm gone."

LONG SILENCE

It was Germanicus who did something stupid while he was gone.

He had the stone clenched tight in his fist – the same fist that was now dripping blood onto the concrete steps. He was not thinking about the fact that the stone had the ability to influence his actions. Sleeplessness, rage and brandy had conspired to deprive him of his rational faculties, and all he wanted to do was destroy. He marched out to the slaughterhouse, picking up a sledgehammer and an iron brick along the way.

CCXXIV

Inside the abattoir our family altar lay in shadow. It was large and flat, made of carved maple with a copper brazier hung above it. There should have been a perpetual flame to Vesta burning, but there were no Vestal Virgins anymore. Germanicus placed the iron block on the altar, and the stone on the iron block, and then he brought down the hammer with all his might. The stone, instead of breaking, flew off and knocked a small hole in the skull of a goat that hung on the wall. Germanicus reclaimed it from the packed earth floor. It wasn't even chipped.

Leaving the slaughterhouse, he went to the shed, grabbed a shovel and marched down a short path into the woodlot. There, in a clearing, was a small graveyard. Its inhabitants included the remains of an unborn child that my mother lost in between Lydia and Juvenal, a small collection of family pets, and a variety of road-kill that Antonia and Catullus had buried because they liked playing funeral. Small limestone headstones were placed haphazardly on the ground, their charcoal inscriptions long since washed away in the rain. Germanicus chose a spot near the base of an old elm-tree and dug a hole. When he'd gone down far enough for the exertion to drain away most of his anger, he dropped in the stone and began to cover it up. Suddenly, unexpectedly, he began to cry – something he had not done since Grandpa's funeral when he was thirteen years old. He fell sobbing on the freshly turned ground, holding on to the shovel as he tried to get back up on his feet. Several large tears watered the earth where the stone had been planted. He wiped his eyes, leaving smudges of dirt across his face.

Finally, he stood. Very formally, out loud, he cursed the square of dirt that held the stone that had consigned his sister to a living death. Then he walked away.

Underneath the earth, in silence, the stone began slowly to put out copper roots.

Thomas met him on the step. "Octavia's leg is a lot worse." He spent a moment gauging my brother's reaction and decided it was safe to continue. "She needs to go back to the hospital."

Germanicus said *nothing*. He said nothing as he loaded me into the car, nothing as we drove to the ER. In the waiting room, he sank himself into his books and ignored me. We waited for hours. Even when they told us that I was going to have to go for surgery, he didn't comfort me – a few minimalist exchanges with hospital staff, that was it. Finally, near midnight, when they came to take me away to the operating room he paused from his schoolwork and kissed me dutifully on the brow. Even now we still weren't talking.

He was equally taciturn when he met me in recovery, even though I babbled on as one does on waking from anesthesia. When the drugs wore off, a thick silence settled between us like a wall of smoke. They released me in the chill hours of the deep night and he wheeled me into the parking lot and loaded me into the car without a word.

We drove home. Germanicus kept almost veering off the road, and when we got to the end of the driveway he ploughed straight into one of my mother's lilac bushes. The door opened into a mass of broken foliage. For a couple of minutes Germanicus stood swaying just outside the car, looking like a surprisingly convincing example of the recently undead.

"Stay here," he said abruptly. "I'll be right back."

I shifted, trying to get more comfortable. Outside, a drizzle of rain had started to fall and the water traced crooked pathways down the side of the windows. The rainclouds shared the sky with a bright full moon.

Germanicus returned with a pillow and a couple of sleeping bags. He opened my door and jammed the pillow in under my head. "What are you doing?" I demanded.

He spread out a sleeping bag over top of me and flicked the child-locks into place. Having sealed me in, he walked around and got back into the driver's seat, pulling the lever so that seat pitched backwards with a dull thunk. It stopped just short of my freshly plastered leg. "Good night."

"We're sleeping out here?"

"Unless you have a forklift." He leaned back his head and closed his eyes.

I wriggled until I managed to find a way of propping my knee up on my brother's headrest. "How can I stop you being mad at me?" There was something I really needed to tell him, but I wanted to wait until he no longer seemed liable to eat my brains.

"Be vexed with no man," he mumbled. It was a quote from one of his favourite Stoic philosophers, and it meant that he was still really angry but trying not to be. Probably it was best to let him sleep.

Outside, I could hear the wind shivering through the trees and the drizzle had ripened into fat raindrops that speckled the roof of the car. I tried to sleep, but the truth was, I was scared. In the hospital, when I'd woken up from the surgery, there had been a woman in the bed next to mine. They left us alone at some point, without remembering to pull the curtain across for privacy. The woman rose up in her bed. Her face was clad in bandages, and all I could see were eyes that starred out of raw, red, blistered sockets. Then she whispered to me the secret of how she had set herself on fire.

Laying back, I tried to forget those eyes.

That was when someone ran into the side of the car.

"Germanicus! Germanicus, wake up!" I was yanking desperately on the interior handle of the door, which didn't open because my brother had locked me in. He stirred, then slowly sat up.

"What's going on?"

"There's someone out there! A child. One of the ones from the Well." I had seen it through the window, pale and feral: a small, gaunt boy with rain running down his face.

My brother fumbled in the glove compartment for a flashlight. He flicked the light on, and for a moment I caught a glimpse of his profile. He didn't look either happy or awake. The car door opened, and I heard my brother's

CCXXVIII

sneaker's splashing through the rain. A chilly beam of light disappeared into the woods.

I pulled the pillow against my chest and hugged it tight. It occurred to me that maybe the boy had been coming to take away the secrets that were gathering inside of me, to bring them to the Well. If I could just get rid of them, then I would be safe. I was locked in, though, and I didn't dare even try to move.

Suddenly, the door behind me opened. I screamed, but my leg was a dead-weight and I couldn't turn around.

"It's all right. Don't panic. You'll hurt yourself." Germanicus was trying to sound steady, but when he stopped speaking his breathing sounded ragged, afraid.

"What happened?" I asked. "Did you find the boy?"

He didn't answer me. "Come on," he said. "We have to get you inside. Now." I could feel his arms shaking with exertion as he lifted me up. Several times on the concrete steps leading up the house he stumbled and once he went down hard on his knee. I heard him gulp back a cry of pain. As soon as the door closed behind us, he collapsed, depositing me on the floor and rolling over in exhaustion onto the hard boards. We stared up at the faces of our household gods. The Buddha laughed. The cold, blue boy scowled his enigmatic scowl. I reached out and took my brother's hand.

"Please tell me what you saw," I pleaded. "You said no secrets!"

Germanicus said nothing.

DAY ??

7:28 – 12:20

Germanicus sits at Dad's desk, propping his head up with one hand as he re-reads the same entry from William's notebook for the 15th time. Next to him are a carafe of cold black coffee (nearly empty), and a journal with a pale blue cover whose pages are covered in the unintelligable markings of Germanicus' private code. The pen that he's holding begins to totter sideways over the side of his hand and he realizes that he's falling asleep again. The other hand jabs a push-pin sharply into his forearm, which is now covered with the scars of his desperate battle against the Dreamlands. In moments of lucidity he's aware that mere pain is no longer sufficient to the task.

He forces himself to stand, heads for the bathroom and turns on the shower. Full blast. Cold. Without bothering to take his clothes off, he climbs in. The shock of the icy spray keeps him on his feet for a few minutes longer. But it fades. He collapses down into the shower, reaching up to turn the tap off, but it's impossibly far away. Crawling out onto the bathroom floor he claws down a towel and stuffs it under his cheek.

His last waking thought is: Octavia is in terrible danger.

10:23 am

Thomas arrives to find a small swamp forming in the hall across from my father's study. He pushes open the bathroom door. Inside, Germanicus lies passed out in soaking wet clothes, his lips blue from sleeping in an icy deluge. Thomas turns the water off. "Germanicus?" Sadly Thomas' character class does not have access to the Raise Dead spell, so Germanicus does not wake up.

Thomas drags him by his feet into the hall and pulls off his wet clothes. My brother is wearing Cookie Monster boxers: a fact that Thomas will remember for later. For now, he wraps Germanicus in a bathrobe, drags him into the games room and deposits him on the shag carpet. Pillow. Blanket. Good.

He checks in on me and finds that for some reason I am sleeping in the armchair, not on the couch. Upon further examination, he discovers that this is because my wrists have been lashed to the arms of the chair. Thomas has only ever heard my account of the altercation between my brother and I, so this strikes him as yet more evidence that Germanicus has become dangerously unstable. He unties me, and gently moves me to the sofa.

I stir a little, open my eyes, smile up at him gratefully. "Thank you," I whisper. He gives me a kiss, and I sink back down into my happy place.

Thomas stays for a while, playing with my hair. There are red marks on my wrists and he rubs them to make them feel better. When he's sure that I'm soundly sleeping he goes and kicks Germanicus. Germanicus groans slightly and rolls over on his side. Thomas kicks him again, but this produces no reaction.

Since Germanicus is clearly comotose, Thomas goes to the front door and whistles. After a few moments a little bundle of matted yellow fur can be seen racing up the drive. Thomas picks up the dog and carries him inside, where he instructs him to guard me while I sleep. Skeeter pricks his ears and assumes the posture of a very small and shaggy sentry. Thomas feeds him a doggy bon-bon and goes home to look after his aunt.

Skeeter smells a cat. He knows that he has a job to do, but also believes cats are a menace that must be put down. He ventures into the hall, sniffing. Isis, seeing that there's a dog in the house, promptly decides on a full frontal assault. Skeeter barks furiously as the cat flies towards him and their bodies collide in a shower of fur. There is a momentary tussle before Isis goes flying up the curtains to hide atop a shelf. In order to make his victory complete, Skeeter goes over to his vanquished enemy's lair and removes an old t-shirt that serves as cat-bedding. For a couple of minutes, the dog violently tears at the shirt with his teeth, chasing it around in circles as a warning. Having made his point, he deposits the t-shirt on a sleeping human's face.

He returns to the study to find that I have gone. He spends a couple of minutes sniffing around, then follows my scent outside. I'm on the drive, slowly dragging my broken body across the gravel. Skeeter can smell blood, and he sees that I've lacerated my knees and torn a long swathe of skin from my arm crawling face-first down the concrete steps. The wounds are deep-speckled with gravel. Skeeter tries his best to clean them with his tongue. I don't react, as if I am not even aware of the dog's presence, as if I don't know where I am.

My guardian tears across the street, yelping for his master. Thomas, who is watching a special about salmon fishing among the Haida of British Columbia, stands and turns off the TV. Skeeter meets him in the doorway and runs circles around his feet, barking with the furious enthusiasm of a dog who knows he's earned a treat.

12:13 pm

Acrid clouds are billowing out of the slaughterhouse door. Thomas's bike skids to a stop and he jumps off leaving the tire still spinning as it falls on its side. The air is greasy with the scent of burning wood and olive oil. He can hear me screaming, but he can't see anything through the smoke. It's Skeeter who is the first to jump forward, sinking his tiny teeth into my collar and making a valiant though futile attempt to drag me out. Using his t-shirt as an improvised gas-mask, Thomas follows the sound of the dog barking as he wades through the choking cloud.

Sometime... Later

I'm lying on the grass. Overhead, I can see big billowy smudges spreading across the bleak cerulean sky. There's a hissing sound, like that of wine poured into a hot cast-iron pan. Thomas is beside me. His body is warm, his breathing heavy.

I reach up, apprehensively, to touch my face, expecting to find a blackened mess. I picture my fingers pulling away from my cheek with a mass of yellow skin clinging to them like cellophane, and then blood pouring down, and the far away sound of my own screams. But my face doesn't even hurt. There's a little pain catching in my chest, that's all.

Confused, I sit up. I can see that my hands are covered in oil, and there's some spilled on my shirt as well. It's only now that I realize that I've just re-enacted another secret. Only this time, instead of dancing on a broken leg and covering myself in marker, I've set the slaughterhouse on fire.

12:18 am

Germanicus starts in his sleep. He's on his feet even before he realizes that he's awoken, pulling on a t-shirt that smells of cat. His jeans are missing, but this crisis is eclipsed by the much bigger problem that he sees through the window. He grabs the phone. 911. Emergency. A fire. They'll be here in 10 minutes? That sounds like forever.

He runs to the study, finds that I'm not there, punches out the window-screen, and jumps through. A few seconds later, he's looming over me on the lawn. "What were you doing?"

"Like before," I say dreamily. "I was someone else."

He hoists me up by the wrist and slings me over his shoulders. I try to kick and struggle, but I feel dizzy, weak. Thomas rises to protest, but Germanicus shuts him down with a look that could split the atom. A paroxysm of pain

CCXXXV

shakes Thomas chest, and he rolls over on his side with a grisly cough.

"Stay still," Germanicus orders. "We're finishing this now."

He carries me towards the graveyard.

In a place out of time

It's still there, just as it was last night when my brother followed the rain-soaked footprints of a forgotten child. Then, it was wreathed in moonlight; now its depths swallow the bright glare of the sun. The Well. Sunken, with jagged teeth rising out of the ground exactly where he planted that stone. He picks up a piece of rose-quartz that marks the final resting place of some long-forgotten pet. He hurls it against the Well-side and retrieves a small shard. "You have a secret," he prompts me, holding up the rosy flake.

I tell him about how I stole the key to my ex-boyfriend's apartment, how I went when he wasn't there and set his bed on fire. How I tripped on the way out, my triumphant vengeance turning into a hideous defeat. With a shudder, Germanicus places the crystal wafer on his tongue, then hands it to me. A moment later, we drop it into the Well. Far far in the distance, sirens can be heard.

INTERVIEW WITH

A ZOMBIE

It is six o'clock and a not especially lifelike Germanicus is sitting outside of an administrative office deep in the bowels of the hospital. It has been four hours since they told him that he would not be allowed to see me.

He looks up and down the hallway, taps his foot on the floor tiles, and tries to be interested in some out-dated Hollywood newsrag which, for some reason, is the only reading material on hand. Nope. He still doesn't care about the lives of the rich and famous even if the news is ten years old. Celebrity gossip doesn't get good until it's aged at least four hundred years.

The door opens. A standard-issue female in a suit walks toward him: brunette, reasonably pretty, trying to look officious. "Kirkman?" she asks. "Let me see if I'm pronouncing this right: Jer-man-i-kus?"

"Close enough. Strictly speaking, it would have been pronounced with a hard g and longer u, but everybody Anglicizes it these days."

His attempt at a joke falls about 175% flat. The woman smiles at him tolerantly, "Why don't you come in."

The office is a cramped space, badly decorated, with a lot of cartoons on the wall that probably make more sense if you work here. Germanicus extends his hand to shake hers, to establish that this is a negotiation. Too late, he realizes that he's wearing a hospital bracelet. He hopes she doesn't ask.

The Administrator-Lady from Central Casting introduces herself, sits down behind a computer, opens a file. "I see your sister has been a regular visitor these past two weeks. When did you say your parents went away?"

He tries to look like the obvious implication hasn't occurred to him at all. "They left on Sunday, not last Sunday, but the week before that."

She nods. The door opens and a second person enters. Male, with short-cropped ash-coloured hair and close-set eyes in a face like a soggy cardboard box. He is very slightly overweight and about twice Germanicus' size. The man offers neither his name, nor any indication of why he is there, but seats himself in the corner of the office next to the goldfish bowl. *Don't mind me*, says his posture, *I'm just here to disembowel you if you answer one of her questions wrong.*

Quickly, Non-Descript Woman runs through all of the same questions that Germanicus has already answered twice before on previous visits. Her eyes keep shifting between his face and the screen: she's checking to make sure his answers today line up with what he said before. He cues the previous conversations in his head and repeats himself, modifying the wording so he won't sound rehearsed.

"Now, you told us yesterday that your parents were on their way home, but their flight has been delayed? So they'll be getting in today?"

His lips slowly retreat from view. "That's not entirely accurate."

"Do you want to tell me what is entirely accurate?"

"I did call them after she broke her leg the first time – but I reassured them that everything was fine. When they asked if they really needed to come home, I said no." He shrugs apologetically, "My sister in Australia just had a miscarriage. It's her fourth one, and she really just didn't seem ready for Mom to leave."

"And did you call them yesterday?"

"I couldn't get a hold of them. Apparently Julia decided she needed to go bury her baby somewhere in the Outback," he figures more detail than that would only make our family look weird. "I don't know. I'll try again tonight."

She looks him over and makes a note. It occurs to him that to her he's just a skinny teenager with huge bags under his eyes who's wearing a ratty t-shirt featuring a Roman Eagle feasting on the entrails of an American Bald-Eagle. "Your sister has a history of mental illness, correct?"

He contemplates rising to my defence, and decides that it's too late for that. With a slight shrug, he throws me under the bus. "We assumed that all of that was over a long time ago. There was an incident when she was ten because a close friend of hers went missing. Since then she's been fine."

"And is there a history of mental illness in your family?" Did her eyes dart towards the bracelet, or is he just paranoid?

"Possibly. My maternal grandmother was pretty strange." He leaves out that Augustus is a basket-case, that Juvenal is probably schizophrenic, and that whatever is wrong with Antonia doesn't even have a name. He also neglects to mention that it's less than three hours since he himself was wheeled off to the ER because someone on the elevator thought he was having a heart attack. That hadn't been his fault: the stairs were out of order.

"So when did you first start noticing that your sister's behaviour was unusual?"

"I don't know," although he feels keenly that what he's about to say is a betrayal, he reminds himself that the wheels of the bus are already going round and round and the only open question is whether he's going under with me. "To be honest, yesterday when she was explaining how she broke her leg *again*... It did seem kind of fishy. But you know, she's my sister. I had to back her up."

Silence stretches as Generica consults the file and makes another note. But when she looks up there is maybe something like a smile lurking around her frosted lips. "The surgeon had noted that he had doubts as well."

Germanicus nods. He's scored a point.

Maybe. She continues, "What I don't understand is why, if you were concerned that your sister might be self-harming, would you lie to the people who would have been able to get her help? Especially since *you* knew your parents *weren't* coming home."

He bites his lip. The silent enforcer stares at him with open hostility and types something into a tablet; it looks as if he might be summoning a swat team to confiscate my brother's head. "I didn't think she was deliberately self-harming. I mean, *I've* re-injured myself before when I thought I was recovering faster than I was. I had..." he shakes his head and decides that maybe this a good time to look like he's on the verge of tears, which isn't hard to fake, because he is. "If I'd had any idea..." He covers his face with one hand and doesn't finish the sentence because he can think of no way to end it that will be both acceptable and true.

A piece of paper slides across the table in front of him. "Well, now that you realize how serious the situation is, maybe you'll share what's actually been going on these past two weeks." A pen comes down on the middle of the page. "I'd like it in writing, and I want you to be as thorough as you can."

Germanicus nods as though he is truly eager to help. Writing is easier than talking. It gives him space to think. "After that, can I see Octavia?"

Any vestige of prettiness is obliterated by the cold, superior line of her lips. "We'll be discussing that with your parents. When we get in touch with them."

She excuses herself, but the human sledgehammer remains. Germanicus closes his eyes and forces himself to breathe. In his pocket, he still has the anxiety meds that he refused to take and it's tempting to just pop them and make the mounting dread subside. He knows that mom and dad are coming home in three days. Meaning he has three days to get me out of the psych ward, repair the mess I've made of the slaughterhouse, and defeat a supernatural evil that has been brooding in the dark since before the dawn of time.

I HAVE A SECRET

Visiting hours were over and Germanicus hadn't come. I'd been relying on him to somehow make this go away, but whenever I asked about my brother they just rearranged my pillows and promised to look into it. I sat up in bed and pulled my good leg up towards my chest. I was scared. No, terrified. People with haunted faces kept walking by in the hall, and every time one of them passed by I wondered what secrets had brought them to this place. If just one of them wandered in and whispered their private burdens to me I could be done for. If the doctors caught me doing anything like I'd done these past few nights they would lock me up for good.

CCXLIII

I resolved to hold vigil. I had my finger near the white button just in case someone who wasn't staff came in. From down the hall, I could see that the lights in the ward were going off and soon I was in semi-darkness, with nothing but the light out by the nurses station and the little electronic blips of colour produced by medical monitors. I asked for water with ice and used the ice cubes to stay awake running the cold, wet surfaces over my eyelids whenever I started to drift.

The hours passed. It's incredibly hard to keep awake when there is nothing to think about, nothing to fix your mind on, nothing to distract you. When you are surrounded by white-noise and the rhythmic hum of machines. When the nurse has made her final rounds and all of the moaners and the groaners, the screamers and the cursers, have been sedated and packed off to sleep. In another ward I might have turned my light on and kept myself busy with a book, but this was psych. I had to pretend to be sleeping or the nurses would give me pills.

It was some impossible hour of the endless night and I had started to drift off in spite of my best efforts to occupy my mind with elabourate imagination exercises that slowly transformed into dreams. I was awakened by the shifting of the curtain next to my bed.

It rippled and I could see a human form pushing against it like a phantom trying to break through a bank of fog to materialize in this world. I stayed absolutely still and didn't make a noise or complain. I was afraid that whatever was there, I would be the only one who could see it, and I didn't want to give the doctors any reason to keep me here. The curtain pulled aside. There was a figure, dressed like me in a formless green hospital gown. I thought it looked like a woman, but the head and shoulders were covered with a pillow case. It tip-toed towards me and bent down at the side of my bed. I closed my eyes and prayed that it was a ghost and not a pervert.

"I have a secret," the voice that whispered into my ear was definitely female. "I didn't really intend to kill myself at all. I just wanted him to know what guilt feels like."

I turned my head ever so slightly towards her. "Who are you?" I whispered. "And why are you telling me this?"

"No names," she said. "I'm going away now. I'm gone." She disappeared back behind the curtain, and I could hear feet shuffling back towards a neighbouring cot.

A second later anothering rustling came from the other side. I reached for the emergency button, but I was paralyzed by the realization that if the nurse did come, I wouldn't know what to say. Another figure was coming towards me. A man this time, I thought, with knobbly knees. His face was covered by an open magazine that showed a picture of Madonna in a knock-off Warhol style. "When God talks to me he sounds like Kermit the Frog." He was gone almost before he had said it.

"I know I'm not really a hybrid," this came from behind an unconvincing hand-drawn facsimile of a grey. "But it's the only interesting thing about me."

There was silence. It lasted just a few moments, and then I heard footsteps again, coming down the corridor towards me. I sat up. This time I was going to be ready. I was going to pull the mask off of whoever it was, and reveal them before they could speak whatever secrets they were compelled to tell.

The curtain pulled aside. I was about to reach out when I realized that the figure was dressed in a nurse's uniform. I sat up, almost crying with relief. "Help me," I said. "People just keep coming to my room." I didn't want to be strapped down, but now that I had these secrets weighing on my chest I knew that I needed to do something so I wouldn't hurt myself.

"Are you awake?" the voice was very quiet as he stepped towards my bed. I gasped. The nurse's face was covered by a surgical mask and a pair of thick, dark glasses. "I have a secret."

YOU HAVE MY
BLESSING

"Is Octavia okay?" Thomas is at the door even before my brother has finished putting his shoes away.

"I have no idea," he shrugs off his sweater and hangs it on a hook.

"Well what did the doctors say?"

"That my blood pressure is through the roof, I'm clinically claustrophobic, and I need to see a shrink. Oh, and that I should take two Xanax and call them in the morning."

Thomas follows my brother to the interior of the house. "I mean about Octavia."

Germanicus turns around and puts his hands on Thomas' shoulders. "Thomas, I'm going to ask you for a favour. I know you are dying of curiosity. But please don't ask me about my sister. Or about any of the stuff that's been going on these past few days. Just be my friend. Tell some jokes or something."

"Can the jokes be at your expense?"

"Sure."

"Okay. I think I can do it then... But it will effect your Stoic-points score."

Germanicus smiles, relieved. "It's okay. The Stoic police are already after me over an incident in an elevator. I'm thinking I'll use the Plotinus defence and say that it was just my poor body that was hyperventilating while my higher self looked on with equanimity."

"Oh yes. The inability to breathe is a great indicator of interior equilibrium. The Philosopher says."

This almost makes Germanicus laugh. He drifts towards the kitchen and starts rummaging around. This isn't the kind day where one can subsist entirely on grapefruits. He's going to need some actual food. "By the way, about Octavia, I'm not holding out on you. I really don't know anything except that she's in the psych ward."

"You didn't get to see her?"

"Not allowed. They don't trust me."

"Mmm. That's very strange. Because, you know, if I arrived to put out a fire in a man's slaughterhouse, and found that he'd just dragged his crippled sister off to the pet cemetery, wearing nothing but Sesame Street boxers, I would think for sure that he was sane."

Germanicus looks at Thomas over the top of the fridge door. "For the record, my actions do in fact make sense."

"Sure. You just want cookie." Thomas does a surprisingly good Cookie Monster voice.

Germanicus doubles over laughing, holding on to the fridge door to keep himself upright. He realizes it's a very long time since he last laughed, and man, does it feel good. "To be fair," he says, "I actually was wearing a shirt."

"Yes. I'm sure it helped that you smell like a cat in heat."

Germanicus goes down. It's a few minutes before he can pull himself together enough to pull a left-over goat leg out of the fridge. The meat is dried out and has definitely seen better days, but he's hungry and he hates to let anything go to waste. He gnaws at it in the manner of a Gaul. "Anyway, the good news is they made me do this exercise where I had to write down, in detail, everything that's happened over the last two weeks. Which meant I had to comb through all of my memories trying to figure out what I wanted to include. And while I was doing that, I came up with a plan."

"What sort of plan?"

"A brilliant one. I mean, probably brilliant. Either it will save everyone: Octavia, William, the lot. Or it will cause a tear in the space-time continuum and all of history will be torn to pieces at the roots."

"You still joking, right?" says Cookie Monster.

"98.7% joking. Mostly I just wanted to take advantage of this once-in-a-lifetime opportunity to sound like Doctor Who."

Thomas looks confused. "I ask because so far I'm not sure all of your plans have gone, you know, as planned."

"I know that. But at this point we're all in. Either we pull this off, or," he raises his eyebrows and flashes a slightly maniacal grin, "zombies eat our brains."

"Mmm." says Thomas. "The hubris and despair combo. Do you get fries with that?"

Germanicus sighs. "Hey. At least if I destroy the universe I don't have to explain to my dad why there are holes in his study wall."

"How much do you trust me?" The Skype connection isn't great, and there's a long pause before the answer comes. My father's face is dark, the light behind him, so Germanicus can't actually make out his expressions beyond the tilt of his head. They converse in Latin, as always.

"That is a question no father wants to hear."

Germanicus has the pinwheel sitting in front of him, planted like a flower in a pot, just to the side of the computer, out of view. "I know. But you're very far away, and there is a possibility that whatever I tell you will be traced."

"Why is that a possibility?"

"I'll have to explain when you get back. Though, obviously if you order me --"

"No. I won't do that."

My brother nods and smiles gratefully. When it comes down to it, there's kind of only so much of the truth that he really wants to tell. "Thank you."

"I would, however, like you to give me an idea of what is going on."

My brother nods. "Octavia is back in the hospital. They believe she's crazy. She's isn't. They also believe that I'm unreliable, and won't permit me to see her. That's why I need to know if you trust me."

"I do trust you. I would still like to know more."

Germanicus lowers his head and rubs the back of his neck. All of the tension that has been building up in his back seemed to have decided on a co-ordinated assault on a single point at the top of his spine. "I understand. I want to be able to tell you more. Honestly." He's surprised to discover that this is a sincere sentiment. Before, he felt confident in his ability to deal with this himself. Now, looking at the outline of Dad's face on a computer screen, listening to his voice coalesce and fragment as it passes through thousands of miles of cable to travel halfway around the world, he realizes just how much he would like the reassurance of knowing that his father actually agrees with what he plans to do. "But it's not worth the risk."

The pause this time is longer than before. My brother and my father stare at each other's images, my brother clearly illuminated by the lamp next to his computer, my father dark, the pictures slightly out of sync. Dad finally speaks, "I trust you. You have my blessing. Now, tell me how can I help."

Germanicus suddenly realizes that if he doesn't end the call right now he's going to start to cry. He turns off the video, just in case.

"I can't see you anymore."

"Give me a second. I'll fix it," Germanicus says in English. Picking up the pinwheel, he plants it directly in front of him in a posture somewhere between prayer and collapse. As soon as he's composed himself, he turns the video back on. "Sorry about that."

"I still can't see you very well."

It's true. Somewhere, in the midst of a distant desert, a storm has blown in and bright-crackling clouds are distrupting the wi-fi at Dad's hotel. "Can you hear me?"

There is a broken, truncated series of sounds, the last remains of Dad's voice, then before Germanicus can explain that Dad needs to call the hospital, the connection drops.

18 000 kilometres away, my father spends a couple of minutes clicking button after button hoping one of them will bring his son back. But they don't.

QUEEN SACRIFICE

"Hi Mrs. O'Hare. Is Catty in?" It's probably too late be knocking on girls' doors unannounced, but Germanicus does not have time to burn.

William's mother's deep-lidded eyes hide behind a pair of stylish glasses. She's edging towards 50 but has gone to a great deal of effort to keep up her looks. Fit, flexible, with flawlessly dyed hair, she has enough sense not to dress like a teen-ager; she dresses like a 30 year old instead. "Germanicus, isn't it?" she asks. "You're one of the Kirkman boys?"

"Yeah. Umm. I borrowed a book from Cataline recently. Do you know if she's around?"

"Well she's in her room. I'm sure she won't mind if you go up."

Germanicus nods a thank you, and proceeds up the stairs. The house smells like new paint. That's the last thing he remembers clearly, but the rest he is able to reconstruct, reasonably accurately he thinks, from fragments of memory, the edges of the gap where events have been.

Arriving at the top of the stairs he enters Catty's room without knocking. She's on the floor, stretched out on a yoga mat wearing a loose grey shirt and a pair of black leggings. She rolls up onto her knees and stares at him, blinking. "Germanicus. This is a surprise. You should have called."

As she slides gracefully to her feet, he grabs her wrist and pulls her towards him. He kisses her hard. Although Germanicus is generally wary of pleasures, when he decides to indulge in them he never does it by halves. If he's going to squander his *dignitas* kissing Cataline O'Hare he's for sure gonna get his money's worth. For a moment she seems frozen, maybe shocked, then her arm winds around his waist and she begins to kiss him back. A minute slides by. Maybe more. Then he pulls back.

He spends a moment composing himself while she stands staring at him, her mouth half open in astonishment. "Okay," Germanicus has restored his passions to their proper place in the pecking order. "Now. I want you to

CCLIV

write that in your diary so you forget it. But I want to you see you do it. I need to understand how it works."

"You what?" Something between anger and incredulity flashes in her eyes, and she makes a sound almost like a laugh. "No way," she says. "That was a great kiss."

Germanicus blinks a couple of times, re-calibrating. "Well... I kind of have a streak going, where I've never really kissed a girl. I've kept it up for 19 years. I don't really want to break it now."

"Then why did you kiss me?" She's wondering how someone so smart could possibly be so stupid.

"Like I said, I need to see what happens when a secret leaves the world. It has to be one of my own, so I can observe it happening. But I'm kind of short of embarassing confessions that I would potentially want to erase from time and space –"

She slaps him, which doesn't hurt very much, but probably he deserves. "Don't toy with me!" she hisses.

Slowly, the degree to which he has miscalculated sinks in. "I'm sorry," he says. "I've been under a lot of stress lately, and I'm..." he tries to think of a way of expressing himself without coming across like a cad. "It's just that the last time I was here, you seemed to be pretty willing to accommodate. And I kind of need your help."

"What for?" She almost spits the words in his face.

"Cataline, I'm really sorry. I didn't mean to offend you. But... think about it. It's in both of our interests for you to write this in your diary now. Because, I mean, it's only a kiss. How good could it be? I'm sure you've been kissed before. You will be again. But you have to admit this conversation is unpleasant, and you don't like to remember unpleasant things."

She narrows her eyes. "Oh no," she says. "This conversation is delicious. Before I only knew that you made a show of being innocent. Now I know it's true." She stares my brother down. "I mean, of course I've been kissed before. By boys that I've forgotten. Boys who've forgotten me. But Germanicus Kirkman's first and only kiss? That, I refuse to forget."

Germanicus studies the board, trying to find any possible move. He can see only one. It's an audacious sacrifice, but one that might, just might, win him the game. "All right," he says, "what if I make you deal? You write this one kiss into your diary, and in return I promise I will do everything in my power to love you for the rest of my life."

A Pinteresque beat passes as Cataline studies him, trying to work out the catch.

"You know my word is good," he adds.

"Yes," she says hesitantly. "I do. I just don't understand how this can be worth so much to you."

He smiles. Plays it cool, "Maybe loving you isn't such a horrible prospect."

She laughs, and they both pretend that they believe what he just said. "All right then," she takes down her diary and a pen. "Consider it done."

When she's finished Germanicus pretends to leave, taking a moment to say good-bye to the O'Hares on the way out. Then he sneaks around the back of the house and climbs up the old maple where the tree house used to be. Cataline opens her window and invites him in. Since he has to keep up his half of the bargain, he can't object when she asks him to sit beside her in her bed. "So," she snuggles up close. "Now do I get a kiss that I'm allowed to keep?"

"Not yet," he says. "Next time. It'll muddy the data if I kiss you again right now."

She rolls her eyes and gives him a faux-whithering look, then curls up with her back to him, still holding his hand. He waits. Eventually she falls asleep, allowing him to extricate himself and take up a position on the garret stairs. He sits there in the shadows, repeatedly refreshing his memory, keeping his eye on the diary like a sniper.

It's very late, probably something like three in the morning, when the window slowly opens and a small figure clambers in. It's clearly a boy, but one so thin and spindly that he looks like a wire hanger from which clothes hang in rags. Hungrily, his hand darts out towards the diary. He takes it down, flips it open, and begins to read out loud. It's clear that he's sounding out the words without comprehension, rushing, stumbling in his haste to devour them from the page. Germanicus can feel his memory being stripped away. He rushes across the room and grabs the book from the boy's hands, seizing the child by the arm. The boy looks up. Their eyes meet. There's a flicker, something long and black in Germanicus' peripheral vision. Before he can identify it, the blade slices upwards cutting deep into his wrist.

With a sharp breath of pain Germanicus lets go. The boy scrambles out the window and is gone. Germanicus stands, the diary tucked under his arm, blood dripping through his fingers onto Cataline's cream-coloured carpet. It's a lot of blood.

He snatches the night-dress out from under her pillow and wraps the wounded wrist up tight. Catty can be heard stirring behind him. The rags of the evening still cling to his memory, and when he opens the diary he can see that only about a quarter of the words are gone. He rips out the page and puts it in his pocket to keep it safe, then returns the book to its shelf.

Well, that went better than expected. Now comes the tricky bit.

OLD

PHOTOGRAPHS

Inside of a small museum, a pool of light spilled out over a long crafts-table, illuminating a collection of old photographs and some yellowed news cuttings. Thomas was flipping very slowly through a file folder, his hands gloved so that the oils on his fingers wouldn't damage the papers. He read slowly, methodically: it was very late and if he wasn't careful then the words would run together and he would miss something important.

Again, he looked at the clock. Three-thirty. He wandered over to the concession stand, took out a key and opened up the refrigerator. Since there was no Mountain Dew left, he settled for a Coke. Quickly, he counted out the cans in the recycling bin. Six, so far. Tomorrow, maybe, he would apologize to his boss and offer to replace them. If there was a tomorrow.

Outside, the wind was making a long shrill complaint to the pine-trees and the river was battering itself against a broken wheel as it tumbled down the mill-race. The wheel drove a single gear, suspended high overhead, which creaked around in a slow, perpetual circle, driving nothing. It was because of the sound of the gutted machinery that Thomas did not at first hear the fist that was beating on the door.

The pounding moved to one of the windows, became frantic. Thomas keyed in the security code and opened the door.

Germanicus stumbled inside and collapsed against a display case. His arm was wrapped in a piece of gauzy, shimmering pink fabric soaked with blood. Thomas unwrapped it and drew a long breath as he gently probed the deep, bloody gash. "I take it," he said, "that things didn't go well with Catty?"

A pale smile. "I don't actually know. I don't remember it very well." They looked at each other. Both understood that this wound needed proper medical attention. Both understood that there was no time, and probably no point.

"I've found a lot," Thomas said, hoping that this would comfort his friend. "Names. Pictures. I mean, we won't know for sure until I talk to Octavia."

Germanicus winced as Thomas swabbed his wrist with rubbing alcohol. "Yeah. Let's just pray they let you in."

☺   ☺   ☺

"I'm her boyfriend. I came to visit and bring her this." Through a gap in the curtain I could see Thomas standing over by the nursing station, holding a small plush owl that clutched a yellow rose in its claws. "Is that okay, or are the patients not allowed to have thorns?"

The nurse laughed and touched the stem of the rose, which had been completely stripped of its natural defences. "I think that will be just fine. She's right in there."

He came in and sat down opposite me. "I brought some pictures," he said. "I thought you might like to see them."

I could tell that the nurse was keeping half an eye on us and I was a little worried. Thomas probably should have made a greater show out of being normal and concerned. I smiled and waved at the nurse, and she turned away and made like she wasn't listening in on us anymore. "I would love to," I said loudly. "You're such a good photographer."

Thomas looked at me oddly and said, "Thank you. But these aren't mine. As you can see, most of them are old. Do any of them seem familiar?"

I began to sort through the faces. The first few just looked like the pioneer children that you always see in books, but then there was a face that I was sure I knew. I couldn't place it, but I put the photograph in a separate pile and continued. As I continued to collect familiar faces, I realized who they were. "These are Antonio's children!" I whispered. "I know them. This," I pointed to a sepia-tone picture of a blond child with a gaping expression and a shirt that was a little bit to big, "He was the boy who was churning the light-press. And this girl. I remember, she was standing in the back holding a toddler, and when she came up to get a kiss she almost blushed." I smiled, stroking the faces in the photographs. It made me feel happy in a way, but sad as well, to see them as real children living in the world.

Thomas nodded. He put a newspaper article down on my dinner tray. "Local child goes missing," the headline read. He looked at me significantly, as though waiting for something to sink in. When it didn't, he drew my attention to a brief line of text:

Dorothy and Graham Lakely are greatly grieved by the loss of their only son, and pray that anyone in the village who has any information should make it known to the authorities at once.

"So?" I whispered, still not getting it.

He reached into his pocket, produced a nickel, palmed it and pretended to pull it out from behind my ear. "They are produced," he said, "like rabbits from a hat. An object of instant sympathy: an unwanted child." He drew my attention back to the newspaper again.

"You mean..." I blinked several times. Thomas couldn't be right. He couldn't. But on the other hand, there was no way that he had made up these stories, written them himself, yellowed the paper, forged the photographs. It just wasn't something he would have done. "Antonio was lying."

"Yes." He put another paper down in front of me, this time a police report from 1923. Then another. And another. Each one described a missing child, like William. He drew my attention to a report where it was recorded that the child had been acting strangely for six months before they disappeared. They were secret-bearers. Not the discarded offspring of their parents' private shame.

"Why didn't the police notice this when they were investigating!" I was angry, but I tried to keep my voice down. "If there had been a string of similar incidents..."

He pointed to the dates. 1897. 1845. Sometimes the gaps between reports were twelve years or more. I nodded understanding. A serial killer or kidnapper would only operate over a single lifetime. This had escaped notice because it had been going on for too long to be the work of a man. Slowly, Thomas began to gather up the photographs. He put them back into the leather folder that he was carrying. He did it so casually, without rushing, that I couldn't imagine how he had known to get the timing right, but sure enough just as he had closed the folder the nurse appeared at the door and peered in. Thomas had taken my hand, and it looked as though we were sharing a completely natural moment of tender intimacy. "I'm sorry," she smiled, "I was just checking in to see if there's anything you need."

I shook my head. "No. Thank you. Privacy, if it's possible at all." She looked at Thomas and I, seemed to decide that he was harmless and we were sweet, and pulled the curtain shut. As soon as she was gone, Thomas' expression began to change. He looked perplexed, concerned. He turned my wrist over. Running down it was a long, jagged scar. I pulled it back and hid it again underneath the sheet. It had appeared in the night and the doctors hadn't found it yet. "A secret?" he mouthed the word.

I nodded vigorously, and suddenly realized that tears were springing to my eyes. I pulled back my hospital robe and showed him other marks, other scars, places where the secrets that had been poured into me last night had inscribed themselves on my flesh.

SACRAMENTAL

ABSOLUTION

"Father?" Germanicus has been knocking for some considerable time on the rectory door when finally it inches open a crack. Father Xu is impeccibly groomed, wearing a dark suit, not quite black, with a collar. He peers out into the early morning with the look of a man who has never quite mastered the habit of saying *Matins* on time.

"Come in," he says. "Come in." Germanicus steps into the hall. The rectory has a kind of empty, echoing sound to it: it's clearly the sort of place that was built to house a small community of priests, but it's since been whittled down to single occupancy.

"What can I do for you?" The priest guides him towards a living room full of beautiful old books. Over the fireplace hangs an image of an oriental Virgin, her head wreathed in cherry blossoms, standing before a mountain with the Christ-child in her arms.

Germanicus shifts awkwardly from one foot to the other. "I want to confess."

Father Xu nods with slow perplexity. This is unexpected. It's a long time since Germanicus has come to him with anything other than purely academic questions about 4th century heresies or the councils of the early Church. "You are not baptized?"

"No. And I don't think I'm exactly ready to commit to something like that. So I understand that it would be contrary to your faith for you to give me absolution. But I'm pretty sure that there's nothing in Church law that would prevent you from listening to me talk."

He nods. This is true. "You have something that's bothering you?"

"No," Germanicus shakes his head. "I just have something difficult I'm going to have to do, and I want to make sure that I don't have any secrets weighing me down."

⊙　　⊙　　⊙

Thomas walked the hospital halls searching for the ideal place. It had to be somewhere with earth. Real earth. It also had to be somewhere that he could go without setting off alarms if he took me for a walk. That was hard to find. Most of the doors led out into horrible concrete courtyards full of cigarette butts. Finally, in the heart of the hospital, he found what he needed. A garden put in many years ago by the children of a local elementary school. Nobody had tended it. The trees were spindly and desperate, straining their skinny trunks up towards the distant sun. The ivy was overgrown. A picnic table suggested that it was only ever used anymore for staff to eat their lunch. He found a place in the corner and bent down, digging at the hard-packed earth with a stick. When he had made a hollow, he took a stone from his pocket and planted it like a seed in the ground. Ideally he would have watered it with his tears, but Thomas was not capable of weeping on demand. When this work was finished he crept back inside.

Nestled inside a plain white envelope is a cheque for ten thousand, six-hundred and twenty-four dollars. Germanicus started saving his money at the age of thirteen when my grandfather passed away, leaving a small inheritance to each of us. He spends money rarely and sparingly, and throughout school he has bagged dozens of scholarships grants and bursaries. Now he is going to give away every single cent of it. The money represents a tremendous sacrifice, literally everything. Years of hard work and self-denial. He takes his pen out of his pocket and writes in angular block caps, *"Sheila Anastasia Waterhouse. With love. GFK.'* Then he walks up to her door.

It's hard not to ring the doorbell, but he realizes that if she comes down and he hands her an envelope, she'll for sure want to open it, and she'll insist that he come in. Sheila can talk for hours and he doesn't have that kind of time. Besides, he doesn't want to have the conversation about whether or not she can accept this kind of gift. Nor, for that matter, does he want the emotional reward of seeing the look on her face. The point here is not to feel good. The point is to make a costly offering in the hopes that the gods will favor him with success.

☺   ☺   ☺

Thomas had promised that he would only walk me around the ward. There wasn't a lot of room, but it didn't really matter. He paced up and down talking about random things like his work at the museum, his second cousin who was getting married, the intricacies of aquaculture, the traditional Maori art of tattoo. Usually he was pretty spare with his words, but now there was an almost regular current of chatter, most of which didn't seem to demand any response. I couldn't figure out why he was behaving this way, until one of the patients in a nearby room started freaking out. I don't know what set him off, but it took four strong men to settle him down. Naturally the ruckus attracted the attention of everyone in the ward. But not

Thomas. He walked calmly past the nurses station, pushed the button that opened the door, and proceded into the hall.

"What are you doing?" I whispered when we were outside. "We'll never get out of here. They'll notice that we're gone. They'll sound the alarm."

"Yes. But it doesn't matter." He was sending a message by text. "We don't have far to go."

☹   ☹   ☹

Nearly there. Germanicus takes the cell-phone from his pocket and reads Thomas' message. There's a second message as well, from Dad, saying that he's in Perth now boarding a plane. If everything goes well, by the time that Dad gets home there will be nothing left to do.

At this point, the apprehension is deadly. Germanicus still has the anti-anxiety meds in his pocket, and also a bottle of brandy, just in case. But his goal is to get through this solely on the strength of willpower, without chemical aids.

To Thomas he responds, "On my way." To our father, just "I love you."

THE BEGINNING
OF THE END

Germanicus was waiting for us in the courtyard, hiding just to the side of the door, out of sight, blowing into the blades of my father's pinwheel and watching as it spun, sending little flecks of coloured light over the dingy courtyard walls. Thomas abandoned the wheelchair at the door, and together they helped me forward over the uneven flagstones. Just above the place where Thomas had planted the stone there was a door. It did not look like the other hospital doors at all, but was wooden with yellow stained-glass panes framed by drooping ivy. The glass hadn't been cleaned in a long time, and it was grimy with dead flies stuck in the corners of the frames.

Inside, there was a breath like an old war hospital where the scent of fear, blood and ancient suffering has settled down in the dust to die. Greenish light came in through old coke-bottle windows, showing a long-abandoned ward with peeling plaster walls. It stretched an improbable distance, rows of old cots with their moth-eaten blankets neatly made and mice moving imperceptibly through the wreckage of the pillows. Dust stirred beneath our feet as we moved across the weathered planks.

Near the end of the ward, the roof had caved in. A splash of yellow light fell in from above, illuminating half of a familiar scene. A sunken Well, emerging out of the splinters of the rotting floorboards. A half circle of mossy stones, and a broken wooden support. As Thomas helped me limp towards it, my brother closed the door.

I knelt down by the Well-side and Thomas handed me a stone. He and Germanicus exchanged glances, but I couldn't even try to work out what they meant. I felt heavy with the leaden weight of all those secrets and I wanted nothing more desperately than to be free of them. I began to tell them, one after another, vomiting them up into the stones. The secrets seemed to have multiplied: there were far more than I remembered. Whenever I finished with one, Germanicus would take the stone from me and Thomas would hand me another.

"Is that everything?"

"I think so."

"Then this one should be the last," Germanicus reached into his pocket and removed a smooth, grey rock. The secret that I had kept, the one that had allowed me to find my way back to the Well.

I leaned my head on the cool stones feeling purged. The scars were gone from my body and I felt like I could sleep for a hundred years. "It's over," I said. I almost felt like I could burst out in laughter or song.

"No," said Germanicus. I looked up. I hadn't realized it until now, but my brother had not thrown a single one of those secrets down into the Well. Instead he was holding them in his cupped hands, a pile of multicoloured pebbles, almost overflowing and spilling on to the floor. Carefully, he transferred the stones to the large pockets of his cardigan. They weighed the sweater down, and pulled the collar across his shoulders like a yoke. He turned to Thomas, "Rope?"

Thomas reached into his jacket and pulled out a long length of slender, silky cord. Large knots had been tied into it at regular intervals. He tied one end around his waist and dropped the other down into the Well.

"Thanks," my brother smiled.

Thomas nodded almost reverently. For a moment they stood looking at one another, and then Germanicus, in an uncharacteristic show of affection, stepped forward and put his arms around his friend. They embraced for just a moment, then patted each other on the back the way that men do to reassure each other that everyone knows they're only friends. "Take care of Viv while I'm gone."

"What do you mean 'take care of Viv'?" I demanded. "What are you going to do?"

Germanicus gestured towards the rope that hung into the Well. Thomas had seated himself cross legged on the ground and looked like he was imagining himself as a tree putting down deep roots.

"This isn't over, Octavia," my brother's tone was grave. "This is just the beginning. If you give these secrets to the Well it will only be hungry for more. And we know what happens to secret-bearers. William was never an exception. He was the rule. He was telling the truth when he said the same thing would happen to you. You know that, right?"

I didn't want to know it, but I did. "You still haven't answered me. What are you going to do?"

"I'm going to go down there and make a deal. These are my currency," he gestured towards his pockets. "These, and this." He held up a sparkly piece of hematite that he'd had since he was a kid.

"What secret is that?" I asked.

"Oh. It doesn't contain a secret. Not yet." He took a step towards me, helped me to my feet and kissed my forehead. "Don't worry," he said. "I won't be long. Wish me luck."

He grabbed hold of the rope. I heard Thomas groan as Germanicus' weight tightened the rope around his waist, but he remained, perfectly still. After about five minutes the rope relaxed. Thomas breathed, rubbing at the places where the cord had cut under his ribs. I looked down. I couldn't see in the darkness, but I knew Germanicus was there. I could hear him breathing, tight, frightened breaths that echoed off the stones.

ATQUE VALE

This is only a reconstruction. A story that I've made out of a fabric of holes. The evidence of a secret ripped from the body of the world. In all important respects it is true. The rest cannot be known.

The bottom of the Well was cold and dark. There was water that rose a little above my brother's ankles, and a musty, unpleasant smell. Claustrophobia came in waves that overwhelmed him. His breathing was shallow and he couldn't get enough air. He curled up, crouching down in the water with his head between his knees. As soon as he was breathing again, he realized his mistake. Already the waters of the Well were rising, curling around him hungrily, reaching for the stones in his pockets. He stood up. "Antonio," he called into the darkness. "I have secrets for you. But if you want them, you're going to have to show your face."

I think he expected that the Well would open out before him. He wouldn't be trapped anymore. There would be a passage – a passage into darkness, sure, but at least a way out. Instead, a figure stepped out of the shadows. Antonio stood in front of him, just a foot away. "I know you despise me, but I do need these for my children."

"Your children wouldn't be here if you hadn't lured them down in the first place." Germanicus's breathing was ragged, but at least he was able to breathe.

"You assume a great deal. Much more than you know."

"Probably," said Germanicus. "I would have liked to have been more thorough. But the Well was torturing my sister, so I didn't have the luxury of time."

I reached out and took Thomas' hand, curling my fingers around his. I'd always assumed that Germanicus was rushing things because he was worried that he would be a failure. Worried that mom would be disappointed in him. I had somehow not seen how difficult it was for him to watch me suffering.

"Should I assume," Antonio's voice was slightly weary, "that whatever you are offering, no negotiations will take place?"

"I do have pretty specific requirements."

"Let me read your mind then. I'm a mentalist, you know," there was a smile in his voice, but not a cruel one. It was almost as though he had seen this kind of thing before. "I sense," he said, adopting a portentous, reverberating tone, "that you are here to offer yourself as secret-bearer in your sister's stead."

I yanked on the rope, momentarily thinking that I would be able to haul Germanicus back out. Of course it was completely slack. Thomas laid a hand on my shoulder.

"Shhh."

"How could you let him?" I hissed.

"Listen."

"Is there a problem with that?" Germanicus was keeping his voice steady.

"If you wish to throw yourself away in a futile gesture, no. I'm sure it will be noble and impressive. But if you think that it will unmake your sister's choice, it will not. She is a secret-bearer. That cannot be undone."

"It seems to me," Germanicus countered, "that if there are two possible conduits through which secrets may leave the world, then it should be possible to regulate which is preferred. I realize that it's not a complete solution. I realize that it would only be a matter of time before the secrets destroyed me and began to flow through Octavia again. But shouldn't it at least provide a reprieve? I mean, William seems to have survived a year before he went under. I think I could at least equal that. Buy her some time."

"Don't you dare!" I shouted down into the wellshaft. "Don't you even – "

Thomas took me by the shoulders and gently pulled me back, holding me tight against him to calm me down. I sort of struggled for a moment, and then realized that I was missing what they were saying down in the Well.

"...but don't be so certain of your endurance. I don't choose children out of cruelty; I choose them because they have fewer secrets to haunt them. The older a person is the more likely that they will rip themselves to shreds trying to undo mistakes, smooth out imperfections." Antonio pulled a handkerchief from his pocket. It was bright red, and it hung limp in the damp, musty air. He shook it once and it fell to pieces, the fibres disintigrating instantly and scattering themselves over the surface of the water. "You may think that I'm evil, but I do a great deal to try to restore my children, to give them whatever happiness is possible here. At your age... I can't say how much I would be able to do."

"I don't care about that. I care about Octavia. And I think you care about getting these secrets. So let's get this over with."

There was a moment's hestitation, and then I heard stones scattering over the surface of the water. Down in the darkness, small hands reached out of unseen shadows, hungry fingers fishing out the precious pebbles from the mud. Then Antonio spoke the words that would condemn my brother to the same fate that I had already accepted for myself.

CCLXXVIII

I was shaking so hard that I could barely help Thomas to pull my brother up out of the Well. When his head finally appeared over the edge of the stone rim I almost wanted to hit him, but he looked so relieved to be out of the close-fitting darkness that I restrained myself to a baleful glare. I was too mad to speak.

Germanicus collapsed on one of the old musty cots, arms outstretched to either side, a cloud of dust and shattered insect skulls rising up beneath him. He laughed. "Step one," he said. "Success." After taking a minute to catch his breath he sat up eagerly on the edge of the bed. "Thomas, you're on."

Thomas nodded. "I have a secret," he said. He stepped forward, and I had the sense that he had deliberately chosen the precise place where the sunlight from the cracked ceiling overhead highlighted a semi-circular smear on the floor. He raised his voice, his hair circling his head like a halo. "In the Beginning," he said, "there was stone and water." He continued, his voice like a long, slow drum-beat as he recounted the history of the Well, leaving out the more fanciful aspects of his earlier account, sticking to what Germanicus would have called the facts. "We do not know how the Well came to this part of the world. We know the names of the secret-bearers who passed into its waters. We know Angela, and Yvette, Brighton and Christopher, Inga and Paul," as he named them, I saw the children climbing up out of the well, as though its hold on them had been diminished. They stood, their slender, pale bodies swaying as they stared in wonder towards the filtered, yellow-grey rays of the sun.

When he arrived at William's name, I felt my throat constricting. I could hear the slapping sound of feet desperately pawing at stone. At last, he emerged, a wraith-like figure so much like the others that for a moment I wasn't certain it was him. "William!" I shouted and tried to get to my feet.

Germanicus grabbed me and forced me to sit back down, "That's not really him," he whispered. "Just a shade. Be patient. You'll be together soon."

Thomas stumbled for a moment over his words, and sorrow flitted like a shadow over his features. He steadied himself and resumed, "and Octavia. These were the lives which the Well claimed for its own. And this is my secret, which I give to you." Germanicus handed him the polished piece of moonstone which Thomas placed briefly on his tongue before offering it back.

"Pretty clever, huh?" Germanicus whispered, reaching for the stone. "Trap the Well in its own mechanisms. Make it's existence into a secret and --" As his fingers closed on the stone he doubled over, falling to one knee in pain. A few small sounds, the tips of repressed screams, echoed in his throat and he grabbed onto my hand as though it were a life-line. Very slowly, with tremendous difficulty, he brought the stone to his lips and placed it on his tongue. He held it there for less than a second before he

CCLXXX

coughed it up, his entire body heaving under the weight of the secret that he had just accepted.

Thomas picked up the stone and handed it back, carefully placing it inside of my brother's tight-clenched fist. He slid his hand in underneath my brother's arm and supported him like a soldier pulling a wounded comrade from the battlefield. Slowly Germanicus rose to his feet. The spectral children formed a circle around them, their eyes wide with hope and terror. Several of them reached out to one another, clasping hands. Perhaps they too had been friends before. The child who had been William took a couple of steps towards me, knelt and slowly curled his small fingers around mine.

"It hurts so much I can't see," Germanicus gasped.

Thomas guided his friend's hand over to the gap in the stones where the side of the Well had collapsed, perhaps ages ago, perhaps when the glaciers had moved across the land. "Right here. Just drop the stone and it'll be finished."

Germanicus gripped the side of the Well, holding himself up. "No," he said. "That wouldn't work. The secret-bearer always remembers the secret. Even when it's been removed from the world, it stays with him." He turned towards us, perching on the edge of the well-side. "I am the Well now. It's here," he struck his breast and grimaced, a slight, involuntary groan breaking from his lips. "I'm sorry, Thomas. I left this part out because I didn't think that you'd agree to it."

CCLXXXI

Thomas' emotions moved like a whale beneath the surface of the ocean, only occasionally visible from the shore. I caught a shimmer of anger, a flash of betrayal, and then a sorrow that broke suddenly from beneath the waves. He pulled my brother to his feet and embraced him. Germanicus clung to him, using Thomas' strength to stand up straight. Neither of them said anything. I guess Thomas knew that it was already too late.

I did not know that. I dropped William's hand and struggled to my feet grasping hold of my brother's arm. "You can't do this! Once you throw the stone away, it'll stop hurting so much. Sure, you'll remember, but what difference does it make?"

He held tight to Thomas' shoulder and turned his head towards me, blinking, trying to get a clear view of my face. "I can feel it inside of me, Viv. I can feel its thoughts. It's working way harder than you possibly could to convince me that I want to stay and go on existing. Because if I exist, it exists, and if it exists then it will find a way to use me to bring it back. And it will corrupt me," he winced, "probably it's already started. I don't have a lot of time, so you'd best just say good-bye."

I glared at him unwilling to accept it. "No."

Germanicus forced a smile. "Don't worry Viv. It's not so bad. Hey, maybe there really are Elysian fields. If so, I'll say hi to Socrates for you."

I threw my arms around him, burying my sobs in his sweater. When I looked up again, I thought I might have caught a hint of a tear glistening at the edge of one of my brother's eyes, but he blinked. It might have been a trick of the light. He let me go, and for a couple of seconds he managed to stand on his own. *"Ave,"* he saluted, *"atque vale."*

He swung his leg over the edge of the Well and for a moment it looked as though he was going to dive down and plummet into the darkness with arms outstretched like Icarus in descent. But a tremor of fear shuddered through his shoulders, and he grasped hold of the rope instead, clinging to it with whitened fingers, and lowered himself down.

Several minutes later, there was a sound of a body falling into the water, and then the small, reverberant splash of a stone.

And the world changed.

EPILOGUE

My name is Octavia. It's a little silly, my parents should have waited until they had eight children to bestow that name, but they only ever had seven, and I guess they really wanted to use it in any case.

It was morning. I was out bathing my feet in the dew, which lay thickly on the grass underfoot and caught itself in the hair of the spider-webs that were strung between the slats of the fence in the front yard.

I heard the crunch of footsteps on gravel somewhere up the road and ran to see who was coming. William was wearing his long coat, which is black and which he wears even when it isn't cold. He had that guilty look on his face that people have when they have just been singing or talking to themselves and think that they might have been overheard. He didn't run when he saw me so I slowed down. We both walked up coolly, and he put his arm through mine.

When we reached the house, he paused in the vestibule, taking the aster from his buttonhole and placing it in the outstretched hand of one of our tutelary deities. It was a weird god made of glazed plaster: a sort of cold blue coloured youth with an over-intense gaze, running at great speed towards an unseen goal with his head turned ever so slightly to look over his shoulder. Today someone had dressed him in a ratty old cardigan which hung off of his slight shoulders and down past his feet like an oversize robe. Grandpa's pipe lay at his feet and a volume of Seneca leaning against his thigh. The flower swayed between his fingers for a couple of seconds and then dropped lightly to the ground. I couldn't understand why anyone had dressed him that way or why he was refusing William's flower, but the gods are often inscrutable.

We went into the kitchen to make a pot of tea. William stood looking out the window at the pond where the geese were slowly paddling around waiting for someone to come and feed them breakfast. I hopped up on the edge of the counter and perched there swinging my legs. "Are we still on for the circus this evening?" I asked.

"Naturally. Why else would I have come."

"I hope there won't be any clowns. I've always been creeped out by clowns."

"There will almost certainly be clowns, Vivi. They will be deliciously creepy."

I jumped down, shrugged on a sweater and sighed. "Well we can't go unless I finish all my chores. I'm supposed to kill a goat today. Actually, I only have to get it ready for the slaughterhouse but I really don't want to do it."

William followed me down to the pasture. Apollo had drawn the sun up into the sky and its warmth was starting to melt the dew. Several kids were skipping towards each other, butting heads, falling over, rolling in the damp grass, and then rising again to repeat their fun. One was standing a little off to the side, nibbling thoughtfully on a bit of weed that was poking through the fence. It was perfectly white and a little over-serious looking.

"Even if you're not actually going to slaughter it, you're going to have make a decision. Which one to choose? Eeny meeny miny mo…" That's William's sense of humor – dark as black coffee or burnt molasses. I smacked him in the arm.

"It's a living thing, and it's going to die."

"I didn't know that you were so sentimental."

I opened the gate to the paddock and went in. There were only three goats that were the right age for slaughtering and it had to be a male – the females we keep for milk. It meant that either one of the ones playing near the water trough or the one munching weeds was going to have to go. I attached a lead to the white one and guided it towards the barn. Here, there was a little enclosure where it would be fed a couple of special treats soaked in wine so that it would be calm when the truck came to pick it up. It rested its head against me, undisturbed, as though it understood what was happening and was willing to trust my judgment.

Suddenly I couldn't move, couldn't leave it there. I went over and rested my head on its back and began to cry. William came over and put his hand on my shoulder. I didn't stop crying, and within a couple of minutes I was sobbing violently, my shoulders shaking, and I couldn't have told you why. "Vivi," he said, "are you okay? You can't actually be this upset over a goat."

"No, I don't think I am," I managed to get out. "It's something else. Something I've forgotten." I picked up my head and looked up. There was a little space above the barn door where I could see the sky outside, high, and wide and blue. I interrogated it for a few moments but whatever I had forgotten, it didn't remember either.

I closed the door to the enclosure and left the goat to sleep. William hooked his arm around mine again and we walked up towards the top of the driveway. The lobelias were in bloom, their fiery heads swaying in the morning breeze. At the end of the drive the flag on the mailbox was up. It shouldn't have been, not on a Saturday. I figured that whoever had last fetched the mail had neglected to put it down, but I checked the box just in case. Inside there was a small envelope with no stamp. It was addressed in blocky handwriting, the kind where all the letters are capitals. I didn't recognize it. "To: Octavia Claudia Kirkman," it read. In place of a return address there were three letters: GFK.

SYMPOSIA

EROS & THANATOS

"...a shaft invincible, in passion's venom dipped" -- Euripides

MELINDA SELMYS

Two series of philosophical dialogues featuring the Kirkman clan. One on sex, another on death.

AGAINST
NATURE

And Other Abominations

HORROR SHORTS BY
MELINDA SELMYS

TALES FROM GRANDMA BO'S COTTAGE

MELINDA SELMYS

www.ingramcontent.com/pod-product-compliance
Lightning Source LLC
Chambersburg PA
CBHW020540020726
47494CB00006B/1852